He tore the oversized shoe from his right foot and stretched out his long toes. Then raked three long grooves into the plastic floor. "What about this, Doc? What about this?"

"Very nice indeed, if I say so myself. I think your claws need trimming."

"The foot needs changing! Am I to go through the rest of my life with a giant chicken foot stuck onto my ankle?"

"Why not? It sure beats a wooden leg."

"I want a real foot!"

His howl went unheard because at that moment there was a loud explosion that blew away most of the roof of the hospital.

HARRY HARRISON

Bill, the Galactic Hero on the Planet of Robot Slaves

A Byron Preiss Book

VGSF

Special thanks to Nat Sobel, Michael Kazan,
John Douglas, David Keller, and Mary Higgs

VGSF is an imprint of Victor Gollancz Ltd
14 Henrietta Street, London WC2E 8QJ

First published in Great Britain 1989
by Victor Gollancz Ltd

First VGSF edition February 1991
Second impression April 1991

British Library Cataloguing in Publication Data
Harrison, Harry, *1925*–
Bill, the galactic hero on the planet of robot slaves.
I. Title
813.53[F]

ISBN 0-575-05003-9

Printed and bound in Great Britain by
Cox & Wyman Ltd, Reading

THE TRUE
STORY OF
BILL

BILL, THAT'S WHAT THEY CALLED HIM. THEY called him that because that was his name. A simple farm boy destined for the stars, ripped from his green acres, his silver robomule, his blue Mom—she had circulatory troubles—and forced by trickery into the armed forces of the Emperor.

The story of how Bill became a Galactic Hero has been told in a book titled *Bill, the Galactic Hero*. It is a true story and there is a tear on every page. (An artificial tear dripped onto the pages by the printer.) Read it. It will make you laugh, make you cry, make you want to rush away and throw up. You will see how hard the military labored to destroy Bill, how he shrunk and withered, then grew and matured under this treatment. Learning, like any good soldier, to curse—say bowb at least 354 times a day—to drink in excess, to lust after girls while his eyeballs bulged with sperm. Any woman would be proud to be his mother. Though I can't think why.

After being drugged and tricked into enlisting in the Space Troopers, Bill was sent for his basic training at Camp Leon Trotsky. It was there under the sadistic guidance of Deathwish Drang, a drill instructor with three-inch-long tusks, that his morale was crushed, his will destroyed, his IQ diminished,

1

his spirit broken as he was turned into the perfect trooper. Only his superb physical condition, the product of years of boring physical activity down on the farm, prevented him from being crushed like a beetle as well. No sooner had his basic training been finished, in fact even before it was finished, and even more important before he could get through the front door of the Lower Ranks Cathouse, he and his bunkmates were bundled off to war aboard the space battleship, the grand old lady of the fleet, the *Fanny Hill*.

The war was on. Mankind was advancing to the stars. For out there among the stardust, suns and planets, comets and space crap, there existed a race of intelligent aliens. The Chingers. They were peaceful little green lizards with four arms, scales, a tail like most lizards. So of course they had to be destroyed. They might become a menace sometime, maybe. In any case—what is an army and a navy for if not to fight war?

The boredom of space service was relieved slightly when Bill discovered that his good friend, Eager Beager, was a Chinger spy. At first this was hard for Bill to understand, even with his militarily lowered intelligence, since everyone knew that Chingers looked like moth-eaten alligators, with four arms, that stood seven feet tall. Bill understood the facts a lot better when he discovered that Beager was a special kind of spy. Well, not really a spy, but a robot operated by a seven-inch-high Chinger from a control center in Beager's skull. Seven inches, seven feet, the military does exaggerate slightly in the need of good propaganda. In any case the spy escaped and the normality of starvation and boredom returned until Bill finally went into battle as a fusetender, tending giant fuses. The battle was fierce, all of his buddies were killed, and Bill was slightly wounded when his left arm was blown off. Despite this, and completely by accident, he fired the shot heard round the fleet—that destroyed the enemy spaceship. A hero now, with a good, strong, black right arm sewed in place of his carbonized left arm (having two right arms he can now shake hands with himself which is lots of fun), he received a medal and a hero's award.

He also managed to go AWOL, which stands for Away Without Leave, also Over the Hill, which is basically slipping out of the clutches of the troopers for a little bit. In the course of his adventures on the planet Helior he also became a spy, got involved in garbage disposal, and other interesting things. So interesting that he ended up in combat and doomed to die on the planet of no return where the troopers went in only one direction. But alcohol-related research revealed that while normal casualties were being sewn up and sent back to combat, new arms sewed on to replace old arms, new everythings, well, almost everything, sewn on as replacements, there was a shortage of feet. A footless soldier would be sent offplanet for repair, to fight another day on another world. Unhappily for Bill he had two good feet and therefore was doomed to die in combat. But, ever resourceful, he blew his right foot off, which was better than getting everything else blown off.

So there it is. With an artificial foot, a growing alcoholic habit, incipient satyriasis, Deathwish Drang's surgically transplanted fangs willed to him, and a hobnailed liver, he is ready for whatever comes. Bill, a trooper loyal to the Emperor, as if he had a choice, destined for life to be an interstellar warrior, since his enlistment is automatically extended whether he likes it or not. About the only thing that he has going for him is the fact that with an artificial foot he has only half as much athletes' foot as the other troopers.

Here he is, a reluctant galactic hero, going into action yet once again.

Harry Harrison

CHAPTER 1

BILL WAS NOT HAPPY IN HIS WORK. HE REALLY should have been since, like most things military, it required little or no intelligence. Just well-conditioned reflexes. Which reflexes now tickled his brain with a reminder that the shuffle of recruit footsteps was growing very dim. He glanced up to see that they were almost out of sight. In fact they really were out of sight behind the cloud of dust kicked up by their weary boots. And their feet were, obviously, weary as well. Bill took a deep breath and blasted most of it out with a single roar of sound.

"To the rear—h'arch!"

A small bird fell to the ground, stunned by the intensity of the command. This cheered Bill ever so slightly since it proved that his skills as a drill-private were improving. It cheered the recruits as well since they were about to march into a deep, rock-filled ravine. The first rank was already atremble with fear, facing the terrible choice of death by falling or death by drill-instructor. They wheeled about, not too smartly since they were stumbling with fatigue, and marched, coughing strenuously, back into the cloud of dust.

As they came closer a snarl of anger twisted Bill's lips, a snarl made even more impressive by the single, long tusk that rested on his lower lip, its yellow tip practically touching his chin. Bill twanged it with his fingernail and the snarl grew snarlier. Two tusks were menacing. One tusk made him look like a bulldog who had lost a fight. Something had to be done about this.

The loud thud of tramping feet drew his attention and his eyes unfocussed to see that the marching recruits were just a step away, the nearest one gasping with fear at the thought of running down the DI.

"Company—HALT!" he bellowed.

Aching feet thudded into silence and the recruit almost thudded into Bill. He stood in shivering eyeball contact with the feared DI, his dusty eyeball touching Bill's bloodshot one.

"What are you staring at?" Bill sussurated with all the menace of a snake in heat.

"Nothing, majesty, sir, your highness..."

"Don't lie—you're staring at my face."

"No, I mean yes, can't help myself since my eyeball is touching your face."

"And it's not just my face you are staring at—it's my tusk. And you are thinking—why has he only one tusk?" Bill stepped back and growled loathingly at all of the swaying, frightened, fatigued, near-death recruits. "You are all thinking that, aren't you? Say *yes!*"

"Yes!" They gasped and croaked in unison, most of them too hammered by fatigue to have the slightest idea of what the hell they were doing anyway.

"I knew it," Bill sighed, then twanged the solitary tusk gloomily. "Not that I blame you. A DI with two tusks would be a fearful and terrible sight. But a single tusk is, I must say it, a pathetic sight."

He sniffled with self-pity and rubbed a pendant drop from his nose with the back of his hand.

"Not that I expect sympathy from you feeble-minded misfits—or loyalty or anything like that, since it is always bowb-your-buddy week. No, I expect raw self-interest and bribery. We will drill until it grows dark or you drop dead, whichever comes first." He waited while the moan of pain sighed through the troops. "Or you might emulate yesterday's intake who, so sympathetic to my problem, freely donated one buck each towards my fang fund. I must admit that I was so grateful that I cut the drill short at that point."

The troopers, all recently and reluctantly drafted into service for the glory of the Empire, had already absorbed a few survival messages. They read this one loud and clear. There was a clink of coins as Bill passed before them and accepted their unsolicited donations.

"Dismissed," he muttered as he counted the loot. Enough, yes, just enough. He smiled and looked down at his feet. The smile instantly vanished. The tusk was only half of his problem. He was now looking at the other half.

His left foot appeared normal enough, encased in its mirror-finished recruit-stamping boot. His right boot was slightly different. More than slightly. For one thing it was twice the size of his left boot. Of even greater interest was the long toe that stuck out through a hole above the heel. An impressive yellow toe that was tipped by a shining claw. Bill growled in frustrated anger and kicked out with his right foot and gouged a deep groove in the hard ground. Something was just going to have to be done about this as well.

Thunder rumbled from behind the mountains as Bill started across the drill field towards the barracks. He cast a suspicious eye at the sky as black clouds boiled quickly into sight. The wind rushed up just as fast as the clouds. He coughed as the dust swirled around him—but not for long. The dust was beaten down by a torrential rain that instantly turned the field to a sea of mud. The rain stopped— as soon as he had been well soaked—and giant hailstones plocked holes into the mud and rattled off his helmet. Before he reached the barracks the clouds were blown from sight and the tropical sun burned billows of steam from his uniform. This planet, Grundgy, had an interesting climate.

This was the only thing interesting about it. Otherwise it was barren and worthless and had only two seasons: frigid winter, tropical summer. There were no minerals worth digging, no land worth planting, no resources worth exploiting. In other words the perfect planet to turn into a military base. This had been done, at great and overpriced expense, until the giant island-continent in the boiling, iceberg filled sea, was a single great military establishment. Fort Grundgy, named after the galaxy-famous Commander Merda Grundgy. He was famous for absolutely nothing other than the fact that he had expired of terminal hemorrhoids from overeating. But since he was the Emperor's granduncle his name would be ever honored.

These and kindred gloomy thoughts sifted through Bill's mind as he sifted through the money-bag in his riveted steel footlocker. Enough, just enough. Six hundred and twelve Imperial Bucks. Now was the time.

He unzipped his boots and kicked them off. The

three yellow toes on his right foot were curled and cramped and he stretched them happily. Then he ripped off his uniform and dropped it into the shredder where the reinforced paper fabric was instantly reduced to its component fibers. He tore a fresh uniform from the roll on the latrine wall and drew it on. He had trouble getting his large yellow toes into his right boot and muttered foul curses as he struggled with it.

It was raining stair rods when he opened the barracks door. Muttering nastily he slammed the door shut, counted to ten, then opened it again and stepped out into the broiling sun and hurried down the company street to the base hospital.

"The doctor is otherwise engaged and cannot see you at this time," the zaftig corporal at reception said as she daintily filed the edge of one blood-red fingernail. "Put your name here for sick call which is three weeks from now at four in the morning— eeek!"

She had eeked because he had growled viciously as he had kicked out with a twisting kick and had torn a groove down the metal of her desk with his clawed heel.

"Don't give me no bowb, Corp, I been too long in the army to take no bowb."

"Apparently you have not been in it long enough to learn any grammar. Out—before I call the MP's and have you shot for destruction of government property—eeek!"

Her pained cry echoed the screech of torn metal as he raked the desk again.

"Call the Doc. Tell him it's about money, not medicine."

"Why didn't you say so to begin with," she

sniffed as he banged the intercom. "Cash customer to see you, Admiral." She did this with alacrity and efficiency since the admiral-doctor was giving her a percentage, as well as a good stupfing, with equal alacrity and efficiency whenever he got his mind off of his illegal experiments.

The door opened behind her and Admiral-Doctor Mel Praktis poked his bald head out and leered one-eyedly at Bill, his other eye hidden by a black monocle. The monocle concealed the fact that the eye had been removed in a manner too disgusting to mention. But had since been replaced by an electronic telescope-microscope, which is a very handy thing to have. His illegal medical experiments had been so loathsome that when they had been discovered he had been condemned to death by impaling— or alternately becoming a medic in the navy. It had not been an easy decision. Though it had worked out well in the end since the alcoholic commander of the base here turned a blind drunk eye on his experiments. Praktis had blinded the eye himself with a limitless supply of medical alcohol to make sure he got away with his dirty work.

"Are you the one for the prefrontal lobotomy?" Praktis asked.

"Not bowby likely. The tusk, Doc, the tusk, remember? I only had enough bucks before for a single implant—but I have the rest now."

"No bucks no tusks. Let's see what you got."

Bill shook the bag so it jingled.

"Inside, we don't have all day."

Praktis shook the coins into the sink, threw the empty bag into the disposal chute, then soaked the money in antiseptic before counting it.

"Never know what grotty infections the troops have. You're ten bucks short."

"You should know—you infected most of them. No bowb, Doc, that's the agreed price. Six hundred and twelve."

"That was last week. I'm taking inflation into account."

"That's all that I have," Bill whimpered.

"Then sign a chit against next month's pay."

"You have no soul," Bill muttered as he signed.

"I checked it at the church when I got in the service. What's the name? I have to access the computer to find where I filed your fang."

"Bill. With two L's."

"Two L's only for officers." He punched the keyboard. "Here it is, under Bil where it belongs. Freezer twelve, in the liquid nitrogen."

He grabbed up metal tongs and rushed off, was back in an instant with a plastic cylinder that smoked moistly in the warm air. He threw it into the microwave and pushed buttons.

"Sixty seconds should do it. Any more and it would be cooked."

"No jokes, Doc. This is a serious matter."

"Only to you, trooper. To me it's just a few more bucks for my broker towards buying my discharge." The microwave pinged and he jerked his thumb towards the operating table. "Take your trousers off and lie down."

"Trousers? It goes in my jaw, Doc—where were you thinking of putting it?"

Praktis's only answer was an evil chuckle as he wheeled the electronic surgeon into place.

Bill gagged as the rubber clamps whipped his mouth open. Praktis muttered and punched commands into the keyboard. Bill screamed hoarsely around the clamps as the laser scalpel sizzled his gums and forceps twisted an incisor.

"Oops, sorry, I forgot." Praktis lied sadistically as he shot in a local anesthetic before continuing. In a matter of seconds the tooth was out, Bill's gum was peeled back, the hole in his jaw drilled larger, the roots of the fang firmly implanted, GrowFlesh pumped into the interstices before sutureglue sealed it all into place.

"Rinse and spit and get out of here," Praktis ordered as Bill climbed groggily on his feet.

"That's better," Bill said, admiring himself in the mirror. He twanged each tusk in turn, then smiled a twisted smile. This was really a very revolting expression. "Deathwish Drang would be proud to see me, if he was still alive."

"Out."

"Not yet, Doc." He tore the oversized shoe from his right foot and stretched out his long toes. Then raked three long grooves into the plastic floor. "What about this, huh? What about this?"

"Very nice indeed, if I say so myself. I think your claws need trimming."

"The foot needs changing! Am I to go through the rest of my life with a giant chicken foot stuck onto my ankle?"

"Why not? It sure beats a wooden leg."

"I want a real foot!"

"You got a real foot—a real giant mutated chicken foot. And let me tell you, not that I want to brag, but there isn't another surgeon in the known universe that could have done that. And they complain about my so-called illegal experiments! They'll

come crawling to me when they have foot trouble—
you wait and see."

"I don't want to wait and see nothing. Except a
real live human foot there."

"You know the drill, trooper, so don't come
whining to me with your petty problems. There is a
war on, soldier—or haven't you heard? There are
shortages. And one thing in really short supply is
spare feet."

"Isn't there anything you can do?"

"I could give you a rabbit's foot instead. They
are supposed to be very lucky."

Bill howled, "I want a real foot!"

His howl went unheard because at that moment
there was a loud explosion that blew away most of
the roof of the hospital.

CHAPTER 2

WHILE DR. PRAKTIS VIBRATED WITH FEAR, gaping vacantly at the gaping hole and falling debris, Bill dived under the metal table. Once his personal ass had been saved he thought of the future, and his chicken foot, so out of pure selfishness reached out and dragged the doctor to safety. A great lump of masonry fell on the spot where Praktis had just been standing and he gurgled with horror. Then bathed Bill with spaniel eyes of gratitude.

"You saved my life," he whimpered.

"Just don't forget that when the next shipment of frozen feet arrive. I want first pick."

"It will be yours! If you are in a hurry I have a very dainty size three foot that was all that was left of a nurse eaten by guard dogs."

"No, thanks. I'll wait. The one I got now has great combat possibilities until Mr. Right Foot comes along."

"Why are you talking about combat?" Praktis squeaked.

"Because we are in it right now. Or don't those bombs, shells, and screams of the dying mean anything to you?"

Praktis's moan of agony was drowned out by a thunderous flapping as a shadow passed over them.

Bill chanced a quick look out from under the table and saw that a ponderous dragon was flying in circles above. The dragon saw his movement with its beady eye, opened its mouth and belched out a tongue of flame. Bill jerked his head back and the smoky fireball sizzled the floor all around them. Praktis groaned and quivered. Bill just felt angry.

"This is no way to run a military base. Where are the defenses? The antidragon guns? I am going to get that scaly mother before it gets me!"

As soon as the dragon had flapped off he scuttled from under the table and dived through the opening where the wall had been. He wasted just one second admiring the great amount of damage that the dragon had done so quickly—then dived for cover again as one of them soared overhead and ejected a stick of bombs from its cloaca. When the last bits of debris had clattered to the ground he rushed to the nearest arms locker and tore the door open with a kick with his clawed heel.

"Great, really great!" he chortled and grabbed up the black tube inside that was lettered SAM in white.

"SAM," he said settling the rest onto his shoulder. "Surface to Air Missile."

His index finger caressed the trigger as he squinted into the sight. A lovely sight of crosshairs on the round belly of the nearest dragon.

"Here's one from the troopers!" he ejaculated happily as he squeezed the trigger.

The SAM clattered and clicked and a metal arm popped out of the barrel with a flag flapping from the end. YOU MISSED was embroidered daintily on the flag.

"This bowby thing is nothing but a training

dummy!" Bill howled and hurled it at him.

But the dragon had caught the motion of the flapping flag and wheeled about in a tight turn. It dived. Smoke blew back from its gaping nostrils as it opened its mouth to exhale the tongue of lambent flame that would cook Bill like a chop on a spit.

"This is it," Bill muttered bravely. "To die so far from home—with a chicken foot."

Closer the flame came and closer—and the dragon blew up as a missile got it right in the belly button.

"At least someone found a SAM that works," Bill grunted as the thing crashed onto the the latrine roof just before him. It made a great clanging sound, instead of the splatting sound that he had expected. This was explained when the dragon's head was torn off by the impact and crashed to the ground. Wires and rods projected from the severed neck, while hydraulic fluid rather than blood spurted from the broken pipes.

"Should have known," he said smugly. "A machine. Flesh and blood dragons are for the birds. Aerodynamically unsound. Wings too small for one thing."

And while he pondered these eternal mysteries he looked on with interest as the top of the dragon's head split and opened like a lid. This was very familiar. Particularly when the seven-inch-high, four-armed green creature looked out at him balefully.

"You are a Chinger!" Bill gasped.

"Well I'm not a dragon's cerebellum if that's what you are thinking," the Chinger sneered.

Bill groped up a chunk of broken concrete to crush the little green bastard but he was too late. The enemy alien kicked open a hatch in the dragon's neck and dragged out a tiny rocket harness which it slipped into.

"Up the Chingers!" it squeaked as tiny rockets flared and it shot off into the sky. Bill dropped the concrete and looked into the control room in the skull. Just like the one in Eager Beager's head, with an operating console and tiny water cooler. There was even a metal label above the commode with a serial number on it. Bill leaned over and squinted at it.

"MADE IN USA, that's what it says. I wonder what that means?"

He wasn't the only one who was interested. Now that the attack was well and truly over, Dr. Praktis came crawling out of the ruins of the hospital. His quivering terror faded as scientific curiosity took its place.

"What on earth is that?" he said.

"Ain't nothing on earth. It is what is left of a bomb-laying, fire-spraying, Chinger flying-dragon machine."

"What does this mean—MADE IN USA?"

"The same question that I was asking, Doc." Bill looked around, then went and dug a gurney from the rubble. "Here, help me load this head aboard and we'll take it to the CO and see what he thinks."

Which proved hard to do since the headquarters buildings had taken a real pasting. An admiral, with the golden fouled anchors and soldering irons of a technical officer on his shoulders, stood staring gloomily at the smoldering remains when they approached. He looked up and nodded at Praktis.

"They missed you and me, Mel, but got all the

other officers. Every one. They were holding an orgy here for a Red Cross benefit."

"At least they died doing their duty."

"A good way to go." The technical officer sighed deeply—then looked very suspiciously at Praktis. "How long have you been an admiral, Dr. Mel Praktis?"

"And what's that to you, Prof. Lubyanka?"

"Because whoever has got seniority is in command. And I have been an admiral for two years, six months and three days come nine o'clock tonight."

"I don't bother keeping track of petty things like that," Praktis sneered.

"Which means you're a short-timer, you butchering medical bastard."

"Circuit-board wiring dingbat!"

"Trooper, kill this mutineer."

"Is that an order, sir?"

"It is."

Bill grabbed Praktis by the neck and began to throttle him. "Finns!... Uncle!" Praktis gasped and the new CO signaled for his release.

"Bring that dragon decapitation with you. We have got to tell Fleet HQ what happened. And find out where this attack came from. This sector was supposed to have been pacified long ago."

Because of its location, behind the sewage treatment plant and distant from the HQ buildings, the electronic lab was untouched. Admiral Lubyanka's engineers hurried to their master's call and carried the dragon debris away. Praktis and Bill were ignored for the moment and, with true trooper's instincts, they scuttled out of sight.

"How about you inviting me to the Officer's

Club for a conference, sir?" Bill insinuated sanguine-ly.

"Why?" Praktis asked suspiciously.

"Drink," was the instant reply.

They were well into their second bottle of Olde Paint Dissolver before the messenger found them.

"Admiral wants you both in his office instantly if not sooner."

"Bowb off!" Dr. Praktis sneered. The messenger drew his gun.

"I was ordered to shoot you both if you gave me a hard time."

The double-time running had sobered them a bit and they stood panting and swaying and holding each other up in front of Lubyanka's desk. He was growling and muttering as he shuffled through the reports before him. He glanced up and shuddered.

"Sit down before you fall down," he ordered, then waved a readout at them.

"SNABU," he grated through gritted teeth. "Situation normal—all bowbed up. Our satellite stations have managed to get an electronic tracer on the track of the spacer that dumped those dragons on us. It headed off in the direction of Alpha Canis Major, a sector which has, up until now, been neutral. We need to know what is going on—and where this planet Usa is."

"Well you are the electronic genius, not me." Praktis sniffed. "There is no work for a tired old sawbones here."

"Oh yes there is. I'm putting you in charge of the pursuit ship."

"Why me?"

"Because you are about the only officer I have left—and rank does have its responsibilities. And

this nerd goes with you since we are short of com-
bat-experienced troopers as well. I'll scratch up a
crew for you—but I can't promise very much."

"Oh thanks a bunch! Any other bad news?"

"Yes. The attack knocked out every spacer we
had. Except for the garbage tug."

"I used to work in garbage disposal," Bill said
brightly.

"Then you will feel right at home. Pack your
bags and be back here by 0315 at the latest. That's
when I send the assassination squad after you. We'll
have the tracking equipment loaded aboard by that
time."

"Any way we can drop out of this?" Praktis
asked gloomily as they picked their way through the
rubble-filled base.

"Not a one. I did the research the first day we
got here. Easy enough to get off the base—but no
place to go after that. Local plantlife inedible. Ocean
all around. No place to hide."

"Whee. Then come with me and carry my
bags."

"You won't need me, sir," Bill said, pointing
behind the doctor's back. "Those three medics
should be able to help you."

Praktis turned to look and saw nothing. Turned
back and saw the same thing. He howled with anger
but Bill was well out of sight.

Out of sight and filled with a sense of dark despair as he shuffled towards the barracks. All right,
the troopers were never a laugh a second, and this
planet was for the pits, but at least he could stay alive
here. But this garbage scow to the stars gig with the
mad doctor in charge had a very bad smell to it. He
groped about in the interstices of his brain cells but

could not find a feasible plan of escape. Blow off the other foot? No, he would end up with two chicken feet—and tail feathers—if he knew Praktis. It looked like it was time for a trip.

Covering the combination lock on his foot-locker with his free hand he punched in the number. Then pushed his thumb against the fingerprint detector plate before using his key. You could never be too secure, not in the troopers. He stirred the contents of the tray with his fingers and wondered what he should take with him on ship. He doubted if he would need the gross of condoms. The knuckle-duster knife with poison darts might come in handy. Something to read? He gloomily flipped through the pages of *Combat Comics:* explosions sounded weakly from its pages, the cries of tiny voices. There was the very good chance, as always, that he would never see this base again. Not that he would miss it. Better take everything then.

Bill dug his barracks bag out from under his bunk and packed carefully by dumping everything from his footlocker into it. There was still plenty of time before he had to board. He touched his sono-watch and it whispered dimly, "Senator McGurk, the trooper's friend, is pleased to tell you that the time is now twenty-three hundred hours." It was a cheap watch, a gift from his mother.

A few hours to drown his sorrows before they left. But he was completely broke. Bill looked around at the empty barracks and wondered who had any booze. Not the recruits, certainly. The sergeant's cell was in the corner and he went and rapped on the door.

"You in there, Sarge?"

The answer was only silence, which was fine.

He wrenched the metal end off the nearest bed and broke the door in. The place was a pigsty—but this pig was a real boozer. Bill selected two of the most lethal looking bottles. Hid one in his barracks bag and cracked the seal on the other. As soon as the steam had stopped rising he drank deep and sighed happily. Before he got too zonked he set the alarm on the sonowatch.

When McGurk, the trooper's friend, told him it was time to wakey-wakey Bill was just finishing the bottle. He staggered to his feet and shouldered his barracks bag. That is he made a feeble attempt to shoulder it, but instead of him pulling it up it pulled him down.

"Wosha," he said, watching the lights go round and round as he leaned on the bag for support.

"You like it down there, sir?" a voice said. After much blinking Bill made out the form of one of the recruits standing over him. Bulging of eye and strong of shoulder. After a few failed attempts to speak Bill managed a coherent and fairly articulate sentence.

"I do not like it down here."

Muttering sympathetically, the recruit helped Bill to his swaying feet, steadied him until he stayed vertical.

"Name . . ." Bill said with slow precision.

"Name's Wurber, your honor. Ahh just arrived . . ."

"Shut up. Pick up that bag. Hold me up. Walk."

In this manner they weaved their way to the landing pad. Bill shuddered at the sight of the battered tug, then permitted Wurber to support him as they climbed painfully aboard.

The recruit's generosity was well rewarded by

his being drafted to load supplies, drafted a second time to fill out the depleted crew. Thus does the military render swift justice to those who break the first commandment:

Keep the mouth shut and don't volunteer.

CHAPTER 3

GIVE HER THAT, THE GRAND OLD LADY OF
the garbage fleet, the *Imelda Marcos,* was a work-
horse, yes she was. Maybe she was wider than she
was long, pitted and rusty, stained black by coffee
grounds, gaily festooned with toilet paper, speckled
with potato peels, maybe she was all those things.
But she could puff and toot and really do her job.
The garbage container had never been made that she
could not lift into space. No sewage tanker existed
that she could not swing into orbit. She was a
worker.

Her commander wasn't. Captain Bly had once
been first in his class in the Space Academy, had had
all of the promise of the best and the brightest. But
he had thrown it all away with one small mistake,
one moment's dallying where he should not have
dallied, one moment's surrender to lust. Unhappily,
his commanding officer had, tragically, returned to
his quarters early that same day. He had found
young Bly in bed with his wife. And his nephew.
Not to mention a sheep, and his favorite hunting
dog. The commander had really loved that dog.

Needless to say things did not go well for Bly
after that. There are some things that are just not
done. Even in the navy. Which says a lot. For a mo-

ment's indiscretion a career had been ruined. He lived to regret it. If only he hadn't taken on the dog too! But it was far, far too late for recriminations. A gentleman would have done the Right Thing. But he was no longer a gentleman. The officers of the fleet had seen to that. He had been shuttled from ship to ship, ever sinking lower, ever moving on. Until he had ended up here in command of the *Imelda Marcos*.

She was a good old tug and did her job with gruff efficiency. Even though her captain was high or stoned, or both, most of the time. But now, for the first time that any of the crew, even the oldest compacter's mate, could remember, he was sober. Unshaven stubble smeared the pasty gray of his jowls, as shaky of hand, bright red of eye, he stood at his post on the bridge and glared at Admiral Praktis.

"You just can't tramp into my ship without a word, weld that great ugly machine to my control console, take command where you are not wanted..."

"Shut up," Praktis implied. "You will do as you are ordered."

Admiral Lubyanka snarled agreement as he pulled his head out of the depths of the machine in question. "And don't you ever forget that, Bly. You take orders from him. You can fly this junker—but Praktis is in command. The electronic tracker is tracking electronically, which is what this entire damn operation is about. My technician here, Megahertz Mate 2nd Class Cy BerPunk, will follow the escaping ship. He'll give you your course. Your assignment, should you decide to take it, and you have no choice, is to track those damned dragons back to their nest—then report the location to me here. Ready, BerPunk?"

The technician soldered one last connection and nodded, his coarse black hair swinging freely over the white pocked skin of his forehead, brushing the black glasses that concealed his eyes. "On line. Systems go," he said coarsely. "RAM is ramming, electrons zinging. All systems go—or already gone."

"And about time too," Lubyanka snarled, then stabbed Praktis in the chest with a sharp finger. "Do this job, Praktis, and do it well—or it's your ass."

"It's already my ass so I have nothing to lose. Heave anchor, Lubyanka, or you will blast off with us to the big garbage dump in the sky. Is the ship secured for takeoff, Captain Bly?"

Bly treated him to a look of withering contempt and cracked his knuckles.

"Good," Praktis said. "I see that we are going to get along real nice."

Bill had to step aside, or rather stagger aside since he wasn't that sober yet, when Admiral Lubyanka made his exit. Captain Bly watched until the spacelock indicator changed from red to green, then thumbed the takeoff warning. The alarm sounded through the ship like a gargantuan eructation and the crew hurried to buckle in. Bill dropped into a vacant seat and pulled the straps tight just as Captian Bly switched on full power. Gravity sat on their chests with the 11G takeoff. Except for Bill who had a rat sitting on his chest as well as gravity, for it had been hurled from the pipes in the ceiling by the blast. It glared at Bill with gleaming red eyes, its lips pulled back by the drag of takeoff blast to expose its long, yellow incisors. Bill glared back, eyes equally red, his yellow fangs equally exposed. Neither could move and they glared in futile hatred until the engines cut out. Bill grabbed for the rat but it leaped to safety and ran out the door.

"We're in orbit," Captain Bly said "What's our course?"

"It's coming, man, coming..." Cy muttered, stabbing buttons and adjusting switches. He sneered at the VDU which was filled with sparkling confetti, then tapped it with a long and dirty fingernail. The image cleared and the trace was clear.

"Time needed. Working it out now. This little old 80286 CPU has got a math coprocessor so it should rustle through the computations like crazy..."

"Shut up," Praktis snarled as he looked around the cabin. Wurber was just starting down the ladder. "You, stop!" he commanded.

"Ahh gotta go to the toilet," he whimpered.

"Your business after my business—and my business is a cold beer. Fetch."

"Got it!" Cy crowed. "Course is right ascension seventy-one degrees, six minutes and seventeen seconds, declination twelve degrees exactly. Hack."

The gyros whined as the garbage tug turned to her new course. Lights flickered and changed on the console under the skilled, if trembling, fingers of her commander.

"Don't unbelt yet," he warned. "The FTL drive, so recently installed, is an experimental model. And this flight is the first experiment."

"Return to base!" Praktis screamed. "I want out!'

"Too late!" Captian Bly chortled in reply, stabbing a button. "Too late by far. We're all in this together—and I have nothing to lose—since I've already lost everything, everything..."

Quick tears of self-indulgence blinded him. But not so much that he didn't see Praktis creep forward to grab him. A blaster sprang into his hand, its gaping muzzle pitted and scarred. "Sit," he commanded. "And enjoy. Up until now Faster Than Light travel has been by Bloater drive. Now, for the first time ever—that I know about—we will be trying out the Spritzer drive. It was installed by that creepo Admiral Lubyanka. Told me that if I would try it out he would clear my name of all shame. Too late! I told him. I live with shame and will die with shame if I must. Now—here we go!"

One grimy thumb stabbed the large red button and a gasp ran through the ship as they felt themselves squeezed in an implacable grip. "That's the ... first part. A black hole has been opened in space in front of the ship. Now we are... being squeezed down... so we can be squirted through the hole at ...FTL speed. That's why it is named the Spritzer drive. We are being pumped under light pressure and spritzed through spa-a-a-ce..."

It was a thoroughly disgusting and uncomfortable way to travel, Bill decided, and yearned for the old Bloater drive. But at least they lived through it, and that was something. When they had become unsqueezed and space outside had returned to normal, Cy turned to his tracker and fiddled with the controls.

"Bang on, baby. The track is still there, stronger and clearer even. And it heads towards that planet you see over there. The one with the concentric rings, an oblate moon and a black spot at the north pole. Do you see it?"

"Hard to miss," Praktis sniffed, "since it is the only planet around. So chart its position and let's get the hell out of here before we are noticed."

"That comes under the heading of famous last words," Captain Bly blubbered, gaping at the viewscreen which was filled with flying dragons.

"Hit the Spritzer drive and let's get spritzing!" Praktis screamed. But even as the words left his lips it was too late. Well before the soundwaves reached Captain Bly's ears it was too late. Lightning bolts of ravening energy poured from the dragons' mouths and engulfed the ship.

All the fuses blew, all the lights went out. And they were falling.

"Getting mighty close to that planet," Bill observed, then drew back before the barrage of curses. "Temper, temper," he said. "Does anyone know how we can get out of this one?"

"Pray," Cy said, rolling his eyes heavenward, or in any direction, which was the same thing. "Pray for salvation and succor."

Captain Bly sneered at that. "You are the only sucker here if you think that is going to help us. We've got one chance and one chance only. Our fuel is gone, our batteries drained..."

"Then we are dead!" Praktis wailed and tore out handfuls of hair.

"Not quite yet. I said we had a chance. The forward hold is filled with garbage and is ready for ejection. This is done by a giant spring that has been coiled up by the compression of the garbage when it was packed aboard. At the very last instant before we crash I will eject the garbage. By the Newtonian principle that for every action there is an equal and opposite reaction our speed will be neutralized and we will come to rest."

"A garbage drive," Bill moaned. "Is this the end? What a way to die..."

But his complaint went unheard for they were already in the planet's atmosphere and the molecules of air pummeled the spacer cruelly. They smashed into the outer skin, heated it into incandescence while the garbage spacer still hurtled downwards. Through thicker and thicker air, through wispy high clouds, towards the ground below that rushed towards them at a terrible pace.

"Fire the garbage!" Praktis pleaded, but to no avail. Captain Bly stood firm. The others added their cries to his, begged and sobbed, but the thick, grubby finger did not descend.

Closer and ever closer they fell, until they could see individual grains of sand on the ground below—

In the final nanosecond of the last microsecond the finger stabbed down.

Ka-chunk! went the coiled spring, releasing its nascent energy in a single mighty spasm.

Ka-flopf! went the garbage, hurtling outward to crash into the planet just below.

Ker-splat! went the space tug as it settled gently into the mound of old newspapers, fish cans, grapefruit rinds, broken light bulbs, beheaded rats, dead tea bags and shredded files.

"Not bad if I say so myself," Captain Bly chortled. "Not bad at all. This is really one for the record books."

The cabin echoed with the click of safety belts being unlocked, the thud of hesitant boots upon the rusty deck.

"Gravity feels good," Bill opined. "A little light, but good..."

"Shut up!" Pratkis snapped. "I have one question and one question only for you, Cy. Did you..." his voice broke and he restored it with a quick cough. "Did you get off the planet's position?"

"I tried to, Admiral. But the power cut off before I could get out a signal."

"Then do it now! There must be some juice left in the batteries. Try it!"

Cy punched in the commands, then thumbed the activator button. The screen glowed—then went black and all the lights went out. Wurber shrieked with fear at the sudden darkness, sobbed with relief when the feeble glow of the emergency blub oozed out.

"It worked!" Praktis chortled. "Worked! The signal went out!"

"Sure did, Admiral. At that strength it must have gone up about five feet at least."

"Then we are marooned..." Bill intoned feebly. "Lost in space. On an enemy planet. Surrounded by flying dragons. Millions of parsecs from home. In a dead spaceship sitting on a mound of garbage."

"You got it buddy-boy," Cy nodded. "That's just about the size of it."

CHAPTER 4

"HERE IS YOUR BEER, SIR. CAN I GO POTTY now?" Wurber gurgled, holding out the once-warm bottle, now blood-hot from his heated grip.

Pratkis snarled an inarticulate reply as he grabbed the bottle and half-drained it in a single glug. Captain Bly groped through the pockets of his crumpled uniform until he found the butt of an H-joint which he lit. Bill sniffed his exhaust fumes appreciatively but decided against asking for a drag. Instead he went to look out of the viewport at this newfound planet, but all he could see was garbage.

Pratkis grimaced as he drained the warm beer from the bottle, then whistled wetly. When Bill looked around he flipped the bottle to him.

"Put this outside with the rest of the rubbish, chicken-foot. And while you are out there sort of have a look-see and let me know what it looks like."

"Are you requesting me to make a reconnaissance and report back?"

"Yes, if that's what you want to call it in your rotten Trooperese. I'm a doctor first and an admiral by accident. So just get on with it."

The dim glow of the emergency light did not penetrate down the ladderway. Bill clicked his heels together to turn on his toe-torch, then climbed down the rungs in the light of his glowing boot. Since there was no power the spacelock would not open when he thumbed the switch. He turned the sticky manual wheel and groaned with the effort. When the inner door had opened about a foot he squeezed through the gap and into the chamber of the lock. A bright beam of sunlight shone through the armorglass window in the outer door. He pressed his eye to it, curious and eager for a glimpse of this alien world. All he saw was garbage.

"Great," he muttered and reached for the wheel beside. Then stopped.

What was lurking beyond the outer door? What alien terrors had the future in store for him? What sort of atmosphere was out there—if there was any atmosphere at all? If he opened the lock he might be dead in an instant. Yet it had to be done sooner or later. There was not much of a future doing nothing, staying locked up in this crumpled garbage can along with its obnoxious captain and the quack admiral.

"Do it, Bill, do it," he muttered to himself. "You only die once."

Sighing unhappily, he turned the wheel.

And stopped when the door cracked open and began to hiss loudly.

But it was only the pressure equalizing, he realized, heart thudding like a triphammer in sudden panic. Wiping the beads of sweat from his brow, he leaned over and sniffed at the draft of air that blew into his face. It was hot and dry—and smelled more than a little of garbage—but he was still alive. After that, feeling very proud of himself and forgetting his animal panic, he kept turning until the door opened wide. Sunlight lanced in brightly and there was a brittle crackling sound. He leaned out to look—turned and went quickly back into the bowels of the ship. Pratkis looked down the ladderwell at him as he ran by.

"Where are you going?"

"To get my barracks bag."

"Why? What's outside?"

"Desert. Just a lot of garbage and sand and nothing else in sight. No dragons, no nothing."

Pratkis blinked rapidly. "Then just why the hell are you getting your barracks bag, Trooper?"

"I'm getting out of here. The garbage is on fire."

Pratkis's scream of pain and shouted commands followed Bill when, equipped with barracks bag, he bailed out through the open door. He did not stop nor even bother to look back. The lesson with the greatest value that he had learned during his years in the troopers was a simple one: cover your ass. He only stopped when he was clear of the tug, threw down his bag and, breathing heavily, sat on a sand dune. Nodding appreciatively, he watched the evacuation of the tug with great interest.

Pained screams and a great deal of shouting and pounding came from the open lock. In a few moments a box of supplies thudded into the sand, to be followed closely by more containers and crates. Since his own survival was at stake he went to help, dragging them clear and going back for more. The flames crackled and grew close. He pulled one more crate to safety then shouted into the ship.

"Anyone getting out better do it now or never." Then jumped aside as the rats deserted the burning ship. After them came the crew, coughing and scrambling for safety away from the flames.

Pratkis was first, of course, since the commander always leads from the front. Particularly during a retreat. Cy was next, staggering under the

weight of some electronic junk, followed closely by
Wurber and Captain Bly. Followed by a stranger.
Not only a stranger, Bill realized, but a strangerette.
A female person with stripes on her arms.

"Who . . . who . . . you?" Bill asked. She looked
him up and down with scorn.

"Knock off the owl imitation, bowbhead, and
say ma'am when speaking to a superior officer. Report. Name, rank and condition."

"Yes, sir—ma'am. Trooper Bill, ma'am, draftee, hungover, tired."

"You look it. I'm Engine Mate First Class Tarsil. Put my suitcase with the rest of the stuff."

"As you command, Engine Mate First Class Tarsil."

"Since we are shipmates you can call me by my
first name. Meta." She reached out and squeezed his
arm. "You got good biceps, Bill."

Bill smiled ingratiatingly as he grabbed up her
suitcase. It was always best to keep on the good side
of the noncoms. Especially female noncoms.
Though, really, he didn't think she was his type. He
liked big girls, but not those a head taller than him.
And her biceps, he pouted with inferiority, were
really much bigger than his.

"Bill," a familiar and loathed voice called out.
"Stop fraternizing and claw your way up here."

Bill joined Admiral Pratkis on the summit of
the sand dune, looking out at the golden majesty of
the setting sun. Which was really the only thing
worth looking at since other than the sun, and the
empty sky with one small cloud that vanished while
they watched, there wasn't anything else.

"Sand, and an awful lot of it," Pratkis said with
an expression of deep gloom.

"That's what deserts are like, sir," Bill said brightly. Pratkis turned a withering glare and scornful sneer upon him.

"When I want that kind of bright Pollyanna bowb I will ask for it. Do you realize the kind of hole that we are in? There is myself and there is you, which is not saying very much. And what else? That dim recruit who was probably a dim civilian yesterday, the captain who is already stoned out of his mind, an electronic technician with no electronics—and that overweight oversexed crewmember who is going to cause trouble, bet on that. We got some food, some water—and little else. I have the intensely gloomy sensation that we are for the chopping block."

"I have a suggestion, sir?"

"You do? Great! Speak quickly."

"Since you are in command and there is a war on—I want a battlefield commission."

"You want *what?*"

"A commission as a third lieutenant. I am an experienced trooper with plenty of service-related know-how—in addition to which I am the only one here with these qualifications. You will need my combat-hardened skills and professional knowledge..."

"Which I will not get unless you have some rank. All right bowb, not that it makes any difference. Kneel Recruit Bill. Rise Third Lieutenant Bill."

"Oh, thank you, sir. That makes all the difference," Bill simpered. Pratkis curled his lip with disgust while Bill dug the tarnished golden pips of a third lieutenant from his pocket and proudly pinned them to his epaulets.

"It is said that every real soldier with guts or talent, or both, marches with a marshal's baton in his pack. My goal is simpler..."

"Shut up. Take your mind off of your pathetic military ambitions and apply whatever intelligence you have, the existence of which I am growing doubtful about, to the problem at hand. What do we do?"

His ambition fired by his newfound rank, Bill hurled himself in to the role with enthusiasm.

"Sir! We will begin by taking inventory of our supplies, which will be guarded at all times and rationed equally among all. When this has been done we will prepare sleeping accommodations for the night, since, as you can see, the sun is setting. Then I will draw up a guard's roster for the night, have a shortarm inspection, prepare battle plans..."

"Stop!" Pratkis called out hoarsely, eyes bulging at the military monster that he had created. "Let's just get our heads together and simply figure out what we have to do next, Lieutenant. Just that much, or it is instantly back to recruit rank with you."

Bill accepted the decision with all the bad grace he could muster up, kicking his clawed heel into the sand and scowling darkly. His military career in command had been brief. He trailed after Pratkis as they went back down the dune to join the others.

"Give me your attention," Pratkis called out. "All of you that is except Captain Bly who has stoned himself unconscious on that cheap drek he smokes. You, trooper, what's your name?"

"Wurber, your highness."

"Yes, Wurber, great to have you aboard. Now go through Captain Bly's pockets and get all the dope he has and bring it to me. When he surfaces he will probably have more stashed, but at least we can start with this. Now listen, the rest of you, we kinda got a problem..."

"You ain't just blowing it out your barracks bag buster," Meta said.

"Yes, well, thank you miss . . ."

"Miss my butt, buster. There are laws against that male chauvinist pig stuff. I am Engine Mate First Class Meta Tarsil."

"Yes, Engine Mate First Class, I fully understand your attitude. But might I also point out that we are far from civilization and all its laws. We are stranded on this unknown alien planet and we will have to work together. So let us abandon our little egos for a bit and try and find a way out of this mess. Are there any suggestions?"

"Yes," Cy said. "We pull a zingo and get out of here. This planet has a magnetic pole."

"So what?"

"So I got a compass. So we can walk in a straight line and not in circles. In the morning we load up whatever food and water that we can carry and split. It's either that or stay here until the natives find us. Whatever you say, Admiral. You're in charge."

The sun set at that moment and stygian darkness descended. Bill turned on his toe-torch and in its feeble illumination they settled down with their problems for the night. The stars appeared, unknown constellations in an unknown sky. It was a time that cried out for strong nerves. Or strong drink. Bill settled for the latter, craftily opened his barracks bag and stuck his head inside and drank from his hidden bottle until he passed out.

CHAPTER **5**

THE RISING SUN WASHED ITS WARM RAYS OVER Bill's sleeping, bristly face. He grunted and opened one eye. Instantly regretted it and slammed it shut with a hideous grating sound as the light punched a hot icepick into his drink-sodden brain. Taking more care this time he rolled over away from the sun, opened his eyes the tiniest slit, then peeked through his fingers. The huddled forms of his shipmates, wrapped like him in GI blankets from the torched tug, still lay in silent sleep. All except for Admiral Praktis who, driven by duty or insomnia, or a full bladder, stood upon the highest dune staring into the distance. Bill smacked his lips and tried to spit out some of the fur that covered his tongue, did not succeed, climbed to his feet and, ever a sucker for curiosity, climbed the dune himself.

"Good morning, sir," he ingratiated.

"Shut up. I can't stand conversation this early in the day. Did you see the lights?"

"Wurgle?" Bill said, gears not meshed, brain still alcohol and sleep sodden.

"That's about what I thought you would say. Listen numb-nuts, if you had stayed alert rather than wallowing in an alcoholic stupor, you would have seen what I saw. On the horizon there, very distant, glowing lights. And no, before you say it, it was not the stars."

Bill pouted because that was what he was going to suggest.

"Definitely lights, waxing and waning and changing color. Get Cy up here. Now."

The technician must have been popping something because he lay unconscious, eyes open but rolled back so that only the whites, or rather the yellows, showed. Bill shook him, shouted in his ear, and even tried a few good kicks in the ribs with no results.

"Really wonderful," Praktis snarled when he got the report. "Is this a crew or an addicts' ward? I'll go give him a shot that will blast him out of it. Meanwhile you stay guard here over this line in the sand so no one walks on it. And don't bulge your eyes at me like that—I haven't gone around the twist. That line points at the lights I saw."

Bill sat and stared at the line and wished he had a drink and fell asleep again—but jerked awake when he heard the ghastly moans. Cy was crawling up the dune on all fours, groaning as he came. His skin was ghastly white and he was vibrating like an electric dildo. Praktis climbed up behind him, his expression one of sadistic pleasure.

"The shot brought him around but, oh boy, has it got some really wicked side effects. That's the direction, juice-head, that line scratched in the sand. Get a fix on it."

Cy dug out the compass, but his hand was shaking too much to read it. In the end he had to lay it flat on the sand. Then he had to hold his head still with both hands to take the sight. After a certain amount of blinking, eye-popping and twitching he spoke in a hollow voice.

"Eighteen degrees east of the magnetic pole. Permission requested to go away and die, sir."

"Permission denied. The shot will wear off soon . . ."

A shrill scream cut through his words, followed by the roar and splat of blaster fire.

"We're being attacked!" Praktis screeched. "I'm unarmed! Don't fire! I am a doctor, a noncombatant, my rank only an honorable one!"

Bill, his brain cells still so gummed by sleep and ethyl alcohol, drew his blaster and ran down the dune towards the firing instead of away from it which, normally, he would have done. He picked up speed, could not stop, saw Meta before him, standing and firing, could not turn and ran into her at full gallop.

They collapsed into an inferno of arms and legs. She recovered first and punched him in the eye with a hard fist.

"That hurt," he whimpered, holding his hand over it. "I'm going to have a shiner."

"Move your hand and I'll give you another one to match. Why did you knock me down like that?"

"What was all the shooting about?"

"Rats!" She grabbed up her blaster and spun about. "All gone now. Except the ones I blasted into atoms. They were getting at our food. At least we know what lives on this planet. Great big nasty gray rats."

"No they don't," Praktis said, having recovered from his fit of cowardice and rejoined the party. He kicked a piece of exploded rat with his toe. *"Rattus Norvegicus.* Mankind's companion to the stars. We must have brought them with us."

"Sure did," Bill agreed. "They bailed out of the spacer even before you did."

"Interesting," Praktis mused, rubbing his jaw, nodding, squinting, doing all the things that indicate musing. "With a whole planet to nosh in—I ask you—why do they come creeping back here to eat our food?"

"They don't like the native chow," Bill suggested.

"Brilliant but incorrect. It is not that they don't like it—there is none of it. This planet is barren of life as any fool can plainly see."

"Not completely, sir," any fool said. Recruit Wurber appeared from out of the desert, his adam's apple bobbing up and down like a yo-yo. He held out a flower. "As soon as I heard the shooting I ran away. Over thataway I found the flowers and . . ."

"Let me have that. Ouch!"

". . . and I cut my hand when I picked it, just like you did just then, Admiral, when you grabbed it."

Praktis held the flower so close that his eyes crossed as he examined it. "Stem, no leaves, red petals, no stamen or pistil. But made of metal. This is made of metal, you idiot. It wasn't growing. It was planted there in the sand by a person or persons unknown."

"Yes, Admiral. Shall I show the admiral where the rest of the flowers are growing?"

He led the way and the others followed. Except for Captain Bly who was still zonked unconscious. Up dune and down dune to a dark patch in the sand where a stand of flowers grew. Praktis snapped one of them with his fingernail and it pinged.

"Metal. All of them, metal." He poked a finger into the damp sand, then sniffed it. "And this is not water—smells like oil." No scientific explanation for the phenomena was forthcoming since he was just as baffled as the others, although he was too pompous to admit it. "The explanation of the phenomena is obvious and a detailed description will be forthcoming as soon as I have completed my investigation. I'll need more specimens. Anyone have a wirecutter?"

Cy did and he snipped off samples as instructed. Meta quickly had enough of this metallurgical horticulture and went back to their camp. And resumed shouting and shooting. The others joined her and the surviving rats fled into the desert. Praktis scowled at the torn open boxes of supplies.

"You, Third Lieutenant, get to work. I want the food repacked and rat-proofed at once. Issue orders. But not you, Cy. I want your help. Over this way."

Bill seized up a torn plastic container of compressed nutrient bars. Known jocularly to the troops as Iron Rations. Even the rats hadn't been able to dent them; broken rat teeth were stuck in the wrapper. After boiling for twenty-four hours they could be broken with a hammer. Bill searched for something edible and a little more tender. He found some tubes of emergency space rations labeled Yumee-Gunge. The others were watching him intently so he passed the tubes around and they all squeezed and sucked and made retching noises. The gunge was loathsome but promised to sustain life. Although the quality of life that it sustained was open to question. After this repulsive repast they worked together in harmony since the pitiful pile of supplies was all that stood between them and starvation. Or thirsting to death, which is faster.

They had just finished when Captain Bly groaned and rolled over, sat up and made dry-smacking noises with his mouth. Bill passed him a tube of Yumee-Gunge and he screamed hoarsely when he tasted it. He alternately sucked and groaned, shuddering the entire time. Praktis appeared and bulged his eyes at the performance.

"Is that stuff really that bad?"

"Worse," Bill said and the others nodded solemn agreement.

"Then I'll pass for the moment. And deliver my scientific report. Those plants with the flowers are alive and growing in the sand. They are not organic carbon-based life as we know it, but are solid metal."

"Impossible," Meta observed.

"Well, thank *you* Engine Mate First Class for the scientific information. But I think that I prefer my rather extensive knowledge to yours. There is no reason why a life form cannot be metal instead of carbon based. I can't for a moment think why it would want to—but let us leave this interesting topic for now and pursue the even more interesting one of our staying alive. Report, Third Lieutenant, food and water status."

"Food, inedible even by the rats. The water should last about a week with rationing."

"Bowb that for a game of darts," Praktis observed gloomily, sat down heavily and stared unseeingly at the metal flower in his hand. "Not much choice. We stay here and starve for a week then die of thirst. Or we march off in the direction of the lights I saw last night and see what's up. Let's see a show of hands. All for staying and dying."

Not a finger twitched and he nodded. "Now—who is for marching out of here?"

The response was the same. Praktis sighed. "I see that the waters of democracy have caressed few fevered brows around here. So let's hear it for the old fascist pecking order. We will march!"

They jumped to their feet, swayed forward awaiting instructions. "You do it, Bill, this must be the sort of thing you were trained for. Divide what we got five ways and fix packs or something that we can carry the stuff in."

"But—there are six of us, sir."

"I issue orders, I don't take them. Five. Report to me when this task is done." He rooted about in Bill's barracks bag as he spoke and emerged triumphant with the remains of Bill's spare bottle of booze. "And while you are doing that I am going to do a little catching up with you teaheads, dopeheads and boozeheads. Work!"

The sun was high in the sky before the job was done. The admiral was snoring happily, the depleted bottle clutched in his limp fingers. Bill pried it away and drained the little booze that was left before waking him up.

"Whuzha?"

"All done, sir. Ready to march."

Praktis started to speak, coughed instead, then held his head in both hands and moaned. "Well... I'm not. Not until I've had a handful of pills." He fumbled through his wallet for a bottle, shook out a dozen tablets and ordered water in a cracked voice. The pharmaceutical dynamite worked its wonders and he finally permitted Bill to help him to his feet.

"Load up. Get Cy over here at once with the compass."

The heavily laden technician staggered up and passed over the instrument, pointing out the heading to be followed. Praktis plugged his pocket computer to a small speaker, mounted this on one epaulet, then searched the digitalized molecular memory for music. Found a merry marching tune, then played it at full scratchy volume while he led his brave little band out into the desert.

As soon as they were gone the rats emerged from hiding, searched what had been left behind for edible remains, then turned their eager attention to the mountain of garbage which was well cooked and finally cooled enough to be consumed. The shuffle of feet and the sound of music soon died away. The only sound to break the desert stillness was the crunch of rodent jaws.

Into this gustatory paradise *something* penetrated. A new sound perhaps, a new presence. Rat after rat lifted its furry head, twitched ears and whiskers. Leapt down from the mountain of mashed munchies and sought shelter.

Something dark and ominous, low and broad and metallic whirred into sight over the top of a dune. Metal clanked against metal and there was a quick burst of sharp bleeping. *Something* passed beside the mountain of steaming garbage, past the burnt out spacer, and slowly up the dune beyond.

When silence once more wrapped the garbage in its pristine mantle the rats reemerged and resumed noshing.

Ignoring the trail of footprints that led away through the sand. A trail now obscured by the tracks of *something* that pursued the valiant little band of survivors.

CHAPTER 6

ADMIRAL PRAKTIS MARCHED PROUDLY AT the head of his brave little band, marching to the jolly drumbeat of the music that was deafening his right ear. Up dune and down dune and up dune once again. Until he looked over his shoulder and saw that he was alone in the desert. His burst of panic was allayed when the first of his straggling followers stumbled into sight. It was Meta striving manfully, womanfully rather, under her load. The others weren't doing quite as well. Praktis sat down and tapped his fingers on his knee and muttered to himself until they had all managed to stagger up.

"We are going to have to do better than this."

"Watch that royal We, Praktis," Captain Bly sneered. "Your We is not carrying packs while our We is."

"You are being subordinate, Captain!"

"You bet your sweet ass I am, sawbones. I was in this man's navy when you were still in premed. We are in a live and die situation here. Probably die. So I don't move until you carry your share."

"This is mutiny!"

"Sure is," Meta said aiming her blaster between his eyes. "Ready for your pack?"

Praktis saw the merits of her argument and only

47

muttered in protest when another pack appeared—
had this been planned from the start?—and was
loaded onto his shoulders. After this redivision of
their burdens they proceeded if not at a smarter pace,
at least at a continuous one. Bill walked in an offcen-
ter and lurching manner because his right foot was
so much bigger than his left. And his toes hurt,
scrunched inside the boot. He wondered why the
hell he was wearing it. Because it had been issued to
him and he would be out of uniform without it.
Fury rose at the thought and he tore off the boot,
hurled it out into the desert and stretched his toes—
sharp claws gleaming in the sunlight. This was more
like it. He hurried to catch up with the others, walking comfortably now.

When the sun was overhead Praktis groaned an
order to halt and they all fell down. Bill, goaded
perhaps by the responsibility of his new rank,
dragged a water container around and doled out a
ration to each of them. Those with strong stomachs
squeezed out a little Yumee-Gunge. Praktis watched
them and tried some himself.

"Yekh!" he retched.

"And you are being complimentary," Captain
Bly said. "It is not edible."

"Something has got to be done," Praktis said
hurling the tube out into the desert. "I was going to
wait—but we need food now or we can't go on."
He rooted in his pack and dragged out a flat case.
"Bill—get me a cup of water."

"What the hell are you doing?" Captain Bly
complained. "You have had your water ration."

"This is not for me—but for all of us. A little
product of my original research. Illegal they said! Le-
gality is for weaklings. All right, there were a few

accidents, not many died, the buildings were rebuilt quickly enough. But I persevered—and won! Here it is!"

He held high something that looked like a plastic-wrapped goat turd. Cy put his finger to the side of his head and made a rotating motion.

"I saw that!" Praktis screeched. "You laugh, just like the rest of them. But it is Mel Praktis who will have the last laugh! Here is a seed, a mutated seed containing growth accelerators never dreamed of by myopic, pedestrian researchers. Watch!"

He kicked a hole in the sand and placed the seed within it, then poured the water over it. There was a puff of steam as the water dissolved the plastic wrapping—followed by a rapid crackling. "Step back! There is real danger."

The ground burst open and green tendrils sprang into the air, blossomed with leaves in an instant. At the same time the sand stirred and rose as powerful roots shot out in all directions. Bill, ignoring Praktis's warning, touched one of the leaves that had appeared almost under his nose. He yiped and sucked his finger.

"Serves you right," Praktis said. "Life and growth generate heat—and at this speed there is far more heat than can be dissipated normally. Look how the ground cracks open as all of the water is absorbed, the sand heated by the burgeoning life within."

It was indeed spectacular. The broad leaves absorbed solar energy to supply the enzyme-driven furnaces wtihin. A thick stem emerged and a gourd swelled out, growing and crackling before their eyes. When it was almost a meter long it grew bright red, sizzled and broke open just as all the leaves and stems turned brown, shriveled and died. The entire process had taken less than a minute.

"Impressive, isn't it?" Praktis gloated as he opened his pocket knife and plunged it into the melon. Steam hissed out and a succulent smell filled the air. "Like lichen, the melon has both animal and vegetable cells within it. The animal cells are mutated beef so that—as you can see—the flesh within has been cooked by the heat of growth so that the melon-steak is ready to eat."

He sliced off a succulent pink slice and popped it into his mouth. Then jumped for safety as the others dived forward.

It was an hour at least before the last chaw was chawed, the final belch belched, the penultimate sigh sighed. Only broken bits of rind remained, while stomachs were filled to the bursting point.

"You got more of those seeds, Admiral?" Bill asked with humble admiration.

"You betcha. So let's dump the iron rations and the rest of the government-issued junk and press on. Let us see if we can reach the lights by nightfall."

There were groans but no real complaints. Even the dimmest of the bunch knew that they had to get out of this desert before their water ran out. Onward they went, and onward still, until the sun was close to the horizon and Praktis called a halt.

"That's enough for today. I think that we are going to have steak again for dinner, so that we may go on refreshed in the morning. And we will get a good sight on those lights tonight.

Tummies full, they sat in a ruminant row on the dune's summit as darkness fell. The first mutters of worry turned to happy shouts as the huddle of lights appeared on the horizon. Strange rays like distant searchlight beams swept the night sky, changing color before flicking out of sight.

"That's it!" Praktis shouted. "And closer too. We'll get there soon, believe me."

They did—and they were wrong. They did not get there the next day nor the one after that. The lights grew brighter but appeared no closer. And the water was half gone.

"We better be halfway there," Bill said gloomily kicking aside the empty container. The others nodded unhappy agreement.

They had eaten their steaks and sipped the small ration of water and it was still early.

"Shall I play some music?" Praktis asked.

He had on the other nights, but tonight no one cared. The gloom in the air was thick enough to cut with a knife. In fact Bill had to cut a bit of it away to enable him to see the others.

"We can tell jokes," he said brightly. "Or ask riddles. What is black, sits in a tree and is deadly?"

"A crow with a machine-gun," Meta sneered. "That one was old when the universe was young. I can sing . . ."

She was drowned out by cries of protest that died to mutters and then to silence. It was going to be one of those nights. So there was a stir of interest when Cy spoke up, for he was ever the silent one, speaking only when spoken to, usually snarling an answer.

"Listen. I wasn't always. Like this. Different. Not as you see now. I led a different life. Two different lives. How it began I have never revealed before. How it ended was tragedy. For I became. Something different. Not proud of it. But it happened. I was a . . . voodooman." His face twisted ob-

scenely as they gasped. "Yeah. I was. I can tell you
of this. If you want."

"Yes, tell us," they cried out and grew close to
listen to—

CY BERPUNK'S TALE

Life for Cy had the taste of a dead cigar butt.

It should. He chewed one. Spit it out. Drained
the dregs of alkpee from the chipped plastic mug.
Dropped it. Crushed it under his spiked heel.

Day of judgment.

Decision.

Outside he blinked in the nacreous light of the
yellow-orange sun. Shards of styrofoam from the
injection works filled the air, turning it into a regurgitant moire pattern.

Time . . .

The crapkicker lolled obscenely against the insanely cracked patterns of the show window. His
skintight bloodsuit sanguinely dripping scarlet
shadows over frenchletters and powderdildos in the
window. He did not look up when Cy came near.
But knew he was there. The jewel encrusted squid,
pendant from one nostril, quivered in anticipation.

"You got?" he grunted laconically.

"Got. You got?"

"Got. Give."

"Good."

The kreditkard, still warm from Cy's body,
changed hands. The crapkicker sneered laconically.

"Reads ten-thousand bukniks. Deal was nine-
thousand. Trying cheat me?"

"Keep the change. Give."

He gave.

The RAMchip, disguised as a peanut, slithered from hand to hand disquietingly. Cy stuffed it cruelly between his lips. Ate it.

"Good."

Gone. Cy was alone. The toothputer accessed the RAMchip. Light and sound rode the starving night. He jumped aside, the vengeful robocab missed. Was swallowed by the strobeshot darkness. No pedestrian was safe in the Spunkk. In the dark alley Cy sought safety behind the overfilled garbage can that compressed under the fatigue of days, discard printout and workweary compchips, derelict discards of onrushing technology, obscenely melding.

Cy ran the RAMchip again.

This was it. Longhidden formula dug screaming from secure RAMbanks. His.

She lay prone on the fukfome bed when he entered. Locked and sealed the door behind him. Stared at her corpsewhite flesh.

"You should get out in the sun more."

No response. Polkadot paint circled her eyes. Blackleather bra and panties, richly adorned with nylon lace, revealed more than concealed her figure. Not good. Too flatchested. No ass.

"Is this room secure?"

"I unplugged the phone."

"Here." He spat the RAMchip into his palm.

"I don't want your lousy secondhand peanut."

Anger flamed an unseen torch behind his eyes. "Dummy. It's the formula."

The computer switched on when he kicked it. An ancient IBM PC, gutted and restuffed with macro Z-80's. Now it had more compergs than a Cray. The RAMchip plugged into the specially peanut-shaped orifice. The screen burst to repulsive life, indecipherable symbols hurtled across it.

"That's it."

"It's indecipherable."

"Not if you have been trained. That is a three, that a seven."

She eyebulged at his arcane knowledge. Turned away, rejected. Popped a pentagon-shaped pill. A Tibetan copy of an illegal Icelandic aspirin. It hit as obscene symbols raced across the screen. The laser printer hummed grotesquely as it regurgitated a printout.

"Here."

"I can't."

"You will. Get everything on the list." He laughed insanely at the smell of aspirin on her breath.

"Drugs. Illegal. Banned." Her fingers trembled with vibratory despair as she read. "Alcohol, distilled water, glycerin..."

"Go. Or you're dead." The muzzle of the .50 caliber machine gun poked its obscene muzzle from his coatcuff. She went.

Cy BerPunk was twenty-one when he marketed the formula. Long lost, forgotten, moldering in the rat-eaten files of the *Amsterdam News*. Now reborn, remarketed, aimed unerringly at the crapkicker market. The newest. The coolest.

Pubic Hair Straightener to go with the latest all-nude craze. Once seen, must be had. And Cy controlled the supply. The bukniks piled up and he watched the zeroes multiply. Until one day...

"Enough!" he exulted unpleasantly.

Now they would let him in. Had to. Their

bankaccount reader checked his balance even as he approached the front entrance of Power House. Many times had he beat feeble knuckles against the chromesteel entrance concealed behind the hologram of a chromesteel entrance. If they read his balance right—he was in. If not—he risked breaking his nose. No danger was too great. His pace never changed.

He stepped through into the lobby. The receptionist wore a holomask that concealed her face. A pig's head stared back at him. A gold ring in her nose, lips redlipsticked.

"Yes," she grunted.

"AppleCore needs me."

Her smile was cold as liquid helium. "Apple-Core needs your money. Voodooman training is not cheap."

"I can pay."

"See Chandu. Room one thousand and nine. Last lift on left."

The door closed and the floor smashed up against his feet. Then against his face as the acceleration flattened him. A thousand stories is a long way to go. When the door slid open sinuously he crawled out. Climbed wearily to his feet. Sucked on a octagonular jellybean filled with caffeine. It tasted repulsive. But he could go on now.

Crashed open the door. Saw the encrusted gleam of chrome machinery, the small man who was their master.

"Shut door. Draft," Chandu ordered as imperiously as the last emperor. His prosthetic left hand whined latinly. It was of Italian manufacture originally designed to open spaghetti pots. He used it to pick his nose obscenely.

"You think you got it in you? Become voodoo-man. A keyboard killer?"

"I know. Don't think. I cut my first tooth chewing a computer mouse."

"Hard do."

"You can do?"

"Nobody can do what Chandu can do. I teach."

The prosthetic slurped with a sound like sucking spaghetti when he pointed to the leering console that almost filled the room.

"80386 CPU. 2 meg RAM. Math coprocessor. Pixel dedicated VDU."

"Forget the basics." He caressed the VDU obscenely. "This is mine. My VDU. I will be a voodooman. Slap the dermatrodes to my skull. Hook me into the circuit."

"To skull? What you smoke? Surging currents from VDU surge your brain to fried mush. Need body to absorb surges. Far from brain. This is suppositrod."

"Suppositrod!" his senses reeled. "You are not going to fix it to my temples? You are going to stick it up my ass?"

"You got it in one."

Now he knew why there was a hole in the seat of the console chair.

But his physical body was forgotten as the current surged succinctly. He was one with the VDU, a voodooman. His senses hurtling through the bowels of the computer. All black, all white.

"Can't you afford color?"

"No believe propaganda," the disembodied voice whispered into the core of his being. "Just for holo ads in subways. Get suckers sign up. All black and white. Needs less RAM."

Cold whiteness of ice, hot redness of red slid from his memory and crashed into empty oblivion. Something loomed from the darkness, came closer, towering out of sight. A skyscraper-size filing cabinet. Made of wood. Covered with cobwebs.

"What gives?" he screamed into the blackshot darkness.

"Gives a filing cabinet. No better way represent computer functions. What you expect? Infinite blue space? Grid of pale blue neon? Color-coded spheres? Bullshit. Holofilm crap for kiddies. How can chemical speed operating human mind follow computer one-hundred thirty million operations a second? Can't. So program written follow what is happening. That program generate this image for slow human brain to follow. Is file cabinet. Open. More file cabinet inside. Open drawer. Find program, card. Go to subprogram. All boring."

"All boring as buffalo chips!" His errant soul roared arrogantly into the susurrating darkness. There was no reply. Chandu had fallen asleep.

Cy learned. It took every buknik he had. And more. He wanted to be a keyboard killer. More than he wanted sex, drink, pot. Wanted it so bad he could taste it. It tasted lousy. He still didn't mind.

But more money was needed. And only one place to get that. In the Spunkk. The subcity below the city. A world aside. Never entered by authority who did not want to wade in the sewer that was the only entrance. Cy waded. Kicked free of the last curl of encoilingly oleaginous water and strode into El Mingatorio. Yellow light the color of a baby's bad dream washed over the clientele. Which was a good idea since most were pretty repulsive. Cy shouldered them aside and slammed his fist on the microscarred plastic of the bar.

"Ouch!" he said. There was broken glass there.

"We're all out of Ouch," the bartender sneered through the sneer permanently painted on his lips. With indeliblepaint. "The usual?"

Cy nodded. Distractedly. He had forgotten what his usual was. The obscenely fat bloated walrus of a man draped across the bar to his left was drinking something that smoked of vile greenness. Not that.

The crapkicker on his right, every obscene spike of purple hair tipped with a tiny condom, was gagging over a glass of smoking purpleness. Not that either.

A glass cracked down before him. Chipping the plastic. "Yours." There was no pity on the barman's lips when he spoke. "Ginger ale."

Cy's sneer matched his as he raised it to his mouth. Drank deep. Felt the rush of revulsion. "You gave me *diet* ginger ale?"

The only answer an obscene laugh like a dying soul that slipped away into the darkness.

In the Spunkk everything was for sale. Cy sold it. Doing anything for the bukniks he needed. Sold his blood. Washed windows. Babysat a two-headed baby. Nothing was too repulsive, too repugnant. He had to. He would be a voodooman.

The day he graduated they came for him.

He could not escape. The windows unbreakable. The door did not stop them.

They broke it down.

"We have you," the first one said, the streetlights through the venetian blinds shining on his face like an obscene polar projection.

"No!"

Was that his voice? Who else's could it be?

"Take it."

The paper was slammed into his reluctant hand, like a poisonous papyrus rattlesnake, rustling like its rattle.

There was no escape. He was drafted.

"I was drafted. I ended up here. A voodooman with no VDU. Wasting my life, my talent. Wiring up circuit boards."

His tears of self-pity dripped unheard onto the sands of the desert. There was only silence as Cy's voice trickled away. The story was done. Not that his audience noticed this since they were all zonked with fatigue, lulled by his voice, all now sound asleep. Not that he noticed this either since he had been popping pills steadily while he talked and was stoned out of his mind. As the last words fluttered down from his lips he fell over into the sand and began snoring.

Nor was he the only one rendering arias of nocturnal harmony. Zizzing and sawing echoed in the still night air for it had been a long and hard day. Yet, hark!, there was also more than snoring here, more of a rumbling and muttering. *Something* black loomed over the top of the dune, its bulk blocking out the stars. It moved forward, hesitated—then pounced. A sudden cry of pain was quickly silenced. The blackness moved away, the rumbling vanished.

Something had disturbed Bill. He opened his eyes, sat up and looked around. Nothing. He lay down and pulled the blanket over his head to drown out the snoring and was asleep again in an instant.

CHAPTER 7

"ON YOUR FEET!" ADMIRAL PRAKTIS shouted, running about and kicking the sleeping forms. Goaded by boot and voice, one by one they raised reluctant heads and blinked at the orange globe of the rising sun.

"Gone. Meta is gone, missing, kidnapped, stolen."

Which was true. They gaped down at the scooped out hollow in the sand right on the spot where she had been sleeping—then goggle-eyed at the tracks that led away from this spot out into the trackless desert.

"Eaten alive by some hideous monster!" Bill wailed, nervously tearing ruts in the sand with his sharp chicken nails. Praktis looked at him with disgust.

"If it was a monster, Third Lieutenant, it had a driving license. Because if I am not mistaken, and I am not, those are tractor tread prints. Not feet, claws, tentacles or whatever."

"Sure are," Wurber agreed, adam's apple bobbing with excitement. "Tractor treads right enough. They're a lot like the old JCB I drove on the farm. Say—do you think there might be a farm near here..."

"Shut up, you moron, or I'll kill you," Praktis hinted. "Something got Meta while she slept. We've got to go after her."

"Why?" Captain Bly grumbled. "She's long dead by now. Not our business."

"Third Lieutenant, draw your weapon. Shoot anyone who disobeys my commands. We will follow the tracks. Load up." He glared at Captain Bly whose complaints muttered away into silence. "Good. Now if you will glance at the compass you will see that the tracks go roughly in the direction we are following. So take everything and let's move out. And quickly."

They moved. Sharing out the contents of Meta's pack and loading up. Bill, his blaster still drawn, took point and led the way.

The sun rose in the sky but they did not stop. They were stumbling with fatigue before Bill called a halt and they dropped in their tracks.

"Five minutes—no longer." Moans of exhaustion were his only answer. Dimly in the distance there was the rumble of an explosion.

"You all heard that," Bill said grimly, climbing to his feet. "Let's move on."

When they had trudged their way to the top of yet one more sand dune they could see the column of black smoke ahead. Bill waved them down and dropped his pack onto the sand.

"Keep your weapons ready—and your eyes open. If I am not back in five minutes..." He opened his jaw, then shut it again, not knowing what came next.

"Look," Praktis said, "just get out there and find out what has happened. If we don't hear from you we'll take it from there."

There was steely resolve in Bill's stride as he marched into battle, down the dune and up the next one. He peered cautiously over the top before he went on. When the smoke was close, just beyond the next dune, he dropped and crawled to the top and with infinite caution peered over it.

"About time you got here," Meta said as soon as his head came into view. "Got some water?"

"Are you all right?" He kept his blaster ready as he crawled forward, looking at the burning metal wreck.

"No thanks to your lot. Let me be kidnaped right out from under your noses."

"What happened? What is that thing?"

"How should I know? What I do know is that I was sound asleep and next thing I'm awake and covered with sand and being tossed about. I sat up and must have hit my head because I was knocked out for a while. I came to, it was black, I could hear an engine and I knew we were moving. I still had my blaster so I shot my way out. Now—the water?"

"With the others." He fired three quick blasts on his blaster. "They'll hear that. Did you kill the driver of the thing?"

"There wasn't one—that was the first thing I looked for. It's a robot or remotely controlled or something. Some sort of machine on treads with that big scoop on the front. It must have scooped me up and trundled off while you all slept so very soundly."

"I'm sorry—but I didn't hear anything . . ."

There was a sharp clang from the other side of the burning hulk, followed by the sound of an engine.

"There's more of them—get down!" he

shouted, setting an example by dropping and burrowing into the sand.

"I'll get the mothers before they get me!" Meta frothed angrily, running forward, blaster ready. Bill reluctantly followed her, hurrying only when he heard the sound of her weapon.

She stood, legs spread wide, blowing smoke from the pitted muzzle of her blaster. "Missed," she said with disgust. "It got away."

Bill looked at the tracks that led up the dune ahead and vanished over the top. They were tiny treads, less than a yard wide, just one set of them. He blinked with confusion. "It went up that way? Then—how did it get down here?"

"It was here all the time, inside this other one," Meta said, pointing at the hinged flap that now gaped open in the side of the wreck. "It came out of here and trundled away and you know, it wasn't a robot driver or anything. It looked just like this wreck, only much smaller."

"We have a mystery here," Praktis said, strolling down the dune as he slipped his blaster back into its holster. "I heard that last—now tell me what happened before."

"Only after some water," Meta said, then coughed. "This has been dry work."

When she had glugged a cupful and repeated her story to everyone's satisfaction they examined the smoldering wreck, kicked its metal sides and admired the massive treads on its tracks. Peeked into the scooplike container where she had been imprisoned. And came away knowing little or nothing.

"You, Cy," Praktis ordered. "You're the technological junky around here. Give this thing a going over while I plant dinner. We'll save some for you."

They were finishing their meal, licking greasy fingers then rubbing them in the sand, when Cy joined them, grabbing up his portion of meat.

"Grerry prenstrating," he said around a mouthful.

"Swallow first, talk later," Praktis ordered.

"Very interesting. This machine appears to have been cast in one piece. No welds or rivets or things like that. And it's completely self-contained. Lots of what looks like circuitry and memory in that bulge up front. Inputs from radar and sonar and what might be an infrared detector. No weapons or anything like armaments. As far as I can tell it just trundles around and loads up the container where Meta got trapped. The drive, that's the interesting part. Solar powered, collectors on top, I think I found big batteries. Then what might be a hydraulic pump and maybe hydraulic lines..."

"What's all this might-be and maybe stuff? I thought you were the technology whizkid?"

"I am. But I'm not going to do much whizzing until I get a diamond saw. Instead of hydraulic pipes there seem to be tunnels in the solid metal for the fluid. Not cost effective at all and I never saw anything like it before. And that's not the only thing different..."

"Spare me the technological breakdown," Praktis grunted. "This little mystery will keep. We have to make tracks after those other tracks of the one that got away. It is also heading in the same direction that we have to go, toward the lights. It may be carrying a message, telling them about us—"

"Telling who?" Bill asked.

"I don't know who or what or which or anything more than anyone else here! All I know is that the faster we move the better chance we have of keeping moving. I would like to find them, or it or whatever, before they find us. So let's get cracking."

For once Praktis got no arguments. He checked the tracks with the compass as they walked, but after a while he put it away. They were going in the right direction. It was a long and hot day yet Praktis did not order a halt until it was almost dark. He scowled at the tracks that vanished into the darkness and Bill came up and scowled with him.

"Are you thinking what I'm thinking?" Bill asked.

"Only if you are thinking that the thing we are following does not have to stop to rest and is scuttling on ahead."

"That was just what I was thinking."

"You better post lookouts tonight. We don't want anyone else getting scooped away in the dark."

They took turns standing guard, not that it was really needed. The sound of engines coming their way was easy enough to hear. They were well dug into the sand on top of their dune, blasters at the ready, while the roar of engines became deafening. From all sides.

"We're surrounded!" Wurber bleated, then yiked when someone kicked him.

But nothing more happened. The engines rumbled louder, then idled down to a background hum. None came close. After a while Bill's curiosity got the better of him and he crawled out for a reconnoiter. There was enough light from the stars for him to make out the dark forms waiting below.

"We're surrounded," he reported upon his return. "Lots of big machines. I couldn't make out details. But they are on all sides, track to track. Should we try and get by them?"

"Why?" Praktis asked with grim reality. "They know that we are here and they have us well out-numbered. If we try to mix it up in the dark we don't know what will happen. Let's sweat it out until daylight."

"That way we can at least see who is wiping us out," Captain Bly sneered as he popped a pill. "I'm opting out. Maybe I'll wake up dead, but at least I won't know it."

No one argued with him. Those who could sleep, slept. Bill tried hard but with complete lack of success. In the end he sat on top of the dune and stared out at their invisible pursuers. Meta joined him and put a friendly arm around his shoulders.

"You are lonely, worried, scared and frightened. I can tell," she said.

"That's not too hard to figure out. What about you?"

"Not me. I'm too tough for that kind of thing. Give us a kiss and forgot all the naughty monsters out there."

"How can you even consider sex at a time like this!" Bill whinnied, shying away from her warm embrace. "We may be dead in a few hours, for all we know."

"What better reason to forget your troubles, dearie. Or don't you like girls?" Her scowl burned through the darkness.

"I like girls, I really do. Just not now. Look!" There was a feeling of relief in his voice as he ejaculated. "Isn't the sky getting light? I better go wake the others."

"The others are all awake," a voice said from

the darkness. "And we were really enjoying the dialogue."

"You're a pack of voyeuristic bastards!" Meta shouted and fired wildly into the darkness with her blaster. But they had dived for cover and no one was hurt. She muttered to herself darkly as the sky lightened, then turned her angry attention to the waiting machines. "I'll get the first one that comes close, right between the eyes. I don't know about you male weakling chauv pigs, but this girl is not going to knuckle under. I'll take as many of them with me as I can!"

"Could we kindly be reasonable about this," Praktis said, from the protection of his foxhole. "Just put the gun down until we see what develops. There will be plenty of time for a shoot-out later if that is the way it breaks."

There was a distant hum and they all looked up as a machine appeared in the sky above. An ornithopter, flapping and fluttering. When it flapped too close Meta sprang to her feet and shot at it. Pieces blew off its tail and it banked sharply and flitted away.

"Oh, well done," Praktis muttered, but not so loud that the angry engine mate first class could hear him. "I would have liked to have kept this thing peaceful."

An engine rumbled to life on the other side of the dune. Meta spun about and got off one shot before Praktis grabbed her.

"Help me!" he shouted. "Before she gets us all killed."

This appeal to cowardice worked and all of the brave men piled on and helped to disarm her. Pretending not to hear what she was calling them.

When they had her gun they moved away and tried to look peaceful and friendly and not worried as the wheeled vehicle ground up the dune towards them. It came close—then turned sideways and stopped. They stepped back as there was a grind of metal— but it was only the doors opening. When nothing else happened, Bill, feeling that his masculinity had somehow been maligned by Meta's superiority, stepped forward to prove that good old macho still wasn't dead. He stopped and looked inside. Turned and reported.

"There's no driver but there are seats inside. Six of them. Just the same number as people we got here."

"A brilliant observation," Praktis said, standing on tiptoe to look into the vehicle. "Anyone for rideys?"

"Do we have a choice?" Bill asked.

"None that I can see." He glanced over his shoulder at the circle of immense vehicles that surrounded them.

"Go for broke," Bill said as he threw his pack inside and climbed after it. "In any case the water is almost gone."

They followed him with great reluctance and suspicion. When they were all seated the doors slammed shut, the engine raced and their pilotless vehicle roared down the hill. A great tank-treaded machine rumbled aside and they shot through the opening and out into the desert. The churning treads threw up a great cloud of dust through which, half-seen, the other machines turned and followed after them.

CHAPTER **8**

"THIS WRECK SURE HAS ROTTEN SUSPEN-sion," Meta said, bouncing about on the metal seat as they hurtled across a rutted ravine.

"But, golly, it sure beats walking!" Bill smarmed, trying to worm his way back into her good favor. Her only response was a lip-curled snarl.

"There's something there, straight ahead," Cy announced, holding onto Wurber's shoulder to steady himself as he stood and squinted into the slipstream. "Can't see what it is—except it looks plenty big."

From a little speck, no bigger than a bird turd, the distant object grew as they trundled towards it. Grew until it was big as a man's hand, grew bigger still until they could pick out details, inexplicable details at first. That remained just as inexplicable as they drew close. As they came over a ridge and trundled down into the valley beyond they could see that the jumble of towers, shapes, structures and such junk, was surrounded by a high wall. The sand here was cut and marked by treadmarks and ruts that crossed and tangled—yet all converged on the same spot—where the wall swelled out into an impressive bulge.

Their vehicle still trundled forward, but the other machines slowed and stopped and remained behind, disappearing from sight in the dust clouds that blew around them. Their transport of delight did not slow as it hurtled towards the wall—which split open at the last moment. They whizzed through the opening and into pitch darkness as the outer wall closed behind them.

"I hope that this thing can see in the dark," Praktis muttered to himself.

Then light appeared ahead and their car slowed, zoomed out into the sunshine and stopped.

"So what's the big deal?" Meta asked. "More sand, a solid wall, and the same sky. For this we could have stayed in the desert . . ."

She broke off as the car doors creaked and snapped open.

"I think they are trying to tell us something!" Wurber said. They got up warily, not that they had much of a choice, and climbed down to the ground. Except for Bill who had even less choice.

"Say, guys, I got a problem. This thing has grabbed me by the ankles."

He stood and pulled, but the metal bands held him fast. And even as he did this, before anyone could turn to help him, the car doors slammed shut. Bill called out hoarsely as the vehicle started forward, knocking him back into the seat. An opening appeared in the wall ahead and they shot into it. The angry shouts of his companions were cut off as it sealed again.

"I'm not sure that I like this," Bill whimpered into the darkness as they rolled on. Through a door and into a sunlit chamber. The restraints slipped free as soon as the car had stopped and the doors opened yet again. Looking around dubiously, he climbed out.

The sun filtered through transparent panels high above, lighting up the complex machines and strange devices that covered the walls. It was all very mysterious but, before he could examine it, a small and bulbous machine on squeaking treads rumbled towards him and stopped. A metal arm with a black knob on the end shot out towards him, would have hit him in the face if he had not ducked. He slipped his blaster from its holster, ready to blow the thing away if it tried to bash him again. But the knob only rotated to face him and remained about a foot from his head. It vibrated a little and made a rasping sound, emitted a high-pitched tone, then spoke in a deep voice.

"*Blep—bleep—bleep-b-blep—bleep!*" it said with electronic enthusiasm, then tilted towards him as though awaiting an answer. Bill smiled and cleared his throat.

"Yes, I am quite sure that you are right," he said.

"*0101 1000 1000 1010 1110*"

"Closer, perhaps."

The thing vibrated—then spoke again.

"*Karsnitz, ipplesnitz, frrkle.*"

"I'm not really catching the drift . . ."

"*Su ogni parola della pronuncia figurate è stato segnato l'accento fonico.*"

"No," Bill said. "I'm still having a bit of difficulty."

"*Vous y trouverez plus million mots.*"

"Not lately."

"*Mi opinias ke vi komprenas nenion.*"

"Getting closer."

"*There must be some language, ugly/squishy one, that you can speak/understand.*"

"Bang on!"

"Does the expression 'bang-on' convey the

meaning that you can comprehend my communication?"

"It sure does. Your voice is kind of gravelly but other than that it's okay. Now I hope that you won't mind but I would like to ask you if..."

The thing did not stay around for a chat but instead rolled backward to the wall and stopped next to a machine that looked like a cross between a TV camera and a water fountain. Bill sighed, waiting for what was to come next. When it came it was most impressive.

Bells rang in the distance and a far-off hooter hooted. All of this grew louder as the wall dilated to form a door, which emitted a golden shaft of light. A golden dais rolled through the opening and came to a halt before Bill. It was covered with golden draperies and upon the draperies lay a golden figure. Roughly human in form, unless you counted the fact that it had four arms, and was apparently made of metal. The golden-riveted head turned to face him, the golden eyelids clicked open, and from the open mouth, complete with real gold teeth, it spoke.

"Welcome, O stranger from a distant world."

"Hey, that's great, you can really talk my language."

"Yes. I just learned it from the linguistic cybernator. But I'm a little unsure about the pluperfect and gerunds. And the irregular plurals."

"I never use them myself," Bill said, humbly.

"Seems like a satisfactory, though more than moronic, answer. Now what brings you to our friendly little world of Usa?"

"Is that what this planet is called?"

"Obviously—dummy, or I wouldn't have said it. As a brief aside, would you by any chance have any advice on subjunctive clauses? Yes, I see, nod your stupid head, you don't use them either. Back to work. Your reason for coming here?"

"Well, our base, which should have been safe if it were attacked . . ."

"That, for your information, is the subjunctive you never use."

Bill, at a loss for words, struggled a bit then went on. "But we were attacked, by giant flying dragons . . ."

"Excuse my interruption, but they weren't, by any chance, giant *metal* flying dragons?"

"Yes—they were."

"So that's what those clanking bastards have been up to!" The golden eyelids clicked quickly and the creature emitted a deep hissing. Then drew its attention back to Bill.

"Do excuse me, I am forgetting my manners. My name is Zots-Zitz-Zhits-Glotz, but you may call me by the diminutive Zots to mark our growing and intimate friendship. And you are . . . ?"

"Recently Commissioned Third Lieutenant Bill."

"Must I use the entire name?"

"My friends call me Bill."

"How nice for you, and them too of course. And I am being a bad host. Is there any refreshment I can offer you? Some refined oil perhaps. Or benzene, well filtered, or a drop of phenol."

"None of those, thanks. Though I could sure use a glass of water . . ."

"You want WHAT?" Zots bellowed with lungs of brass. "Or, ha-ha, perhaps I did not hear you right. You might possibly want some substance that I have never heard of. You would not have asked for *water,* the liquid form of the compound H_2O, at this temperature, containing two molecules of hydrogen to one of oxygen?"

"That's it, that's what I want, Mr. Zots. Your chemistry is sure good!"

"Guards! Destroy this creature! It wants to assassinate me, poison me! Decog it! Melt it down! Loosen its nuts!"

Bill drew back, whinnying with fear, as a frightening selection of ambulatory hardware crashed towards him. The pincers, metal claws, writhing tentacles, spud wrenches, were just about to grab and rend him when the voice rang out one more time.

"Stop!"

They all stopped in midattack. Except for one machine with extending arms that had been extended too far. It tilted forward and crashed to the floor.

"A single question, squishy stranger Bill, before I unleash the hordes yet one more time. This water —what had you planned to do with it?"

"Why drink it of course. I'm really thirsty." A metal shiver passed over Zots's golden figure. Bill, for one of the few times in his life, had an original idea. With apparently great effort, over an extended period of time, his militarily decayed braincells had added up two and two and managed to get four.

"I *like* water. Why, ninety-five percent of my body," he said, getting it wrong, "is made up of water."

"Will wonders never cease!" Zots dropped back onto his drapes and cogitated so hard you could hear the wheels turning. "Guards, retreat," he ordered, and they did. "I suppose it is theoretically possible to have a life form based on water, though it sounds disgusting."

"Not water, really," Bill said, dredging around for long-forgotten science lessons. "But carbon, that's it. And chlorophyll, you know the kind of thing."

"No, frankly, I don't. But I am a quick read."

"Now can I ask one?" He took Zots's languid nod for assent. "I'm just guessing. But you are made of metal. Not made, you *are* metal."

"That seems rather obvious."

"Then you are a living metal machine!"

"I take affront at the word machine used in this context. Metal-based life form would be more precise. We must have a good chat about this, and flying dragons, other topics of great interest. But first, here is your poison—I *do* beg your pardon—beverage."

A metal platform rolled forward, stretched out an extending arm and deposited a glass receptacle on the floor before Bill. It retreated quickly. Bill picked it up and saw that a transparent liquid was gurgling about inside. With some difficulty he found the seal and the top finally snapped open. He sniffed suspiciously but could smell nothing. Dipped the tip of one finger into it, felt nothing. Licked the finger.

"That's good old H_2O, Zots good buddy, thanks a million."

He gurgled and gasped and drained the vessel, lowering it with a satisfied Ahhh.

"Now I have seen everything . . ." Zots breathed with awe in his voice. "Have I really got something to tell the boys down at the machine shop." He snapped his fingers and a wheeled and tentacled device rolled forward and handed him a can of oil. He held it out in a toast. "Here's to you, O poison-drinking alien." He drained it and tossed it aside. "Enough sociality—to work. You must tell me more about the attack of the flying dragons. Do you know why they should want to do this?"

"You bet I do. The attack was directed by the vile and disgusting Chingers."

"This story gets better and better. What exactly is a Chinger?"

"They are the enemy."

"Of *who?*"

"Mankind. That is me, I mean we, people. These Chingers are an alien and intelligent species that wants to destroy us. So naturally we have to destroy them first. Destruction on a large scale is called war."

"Understanding penetrates. You and your other watery-squashy folk are at war with these Chingers. Might I ask—is their metabolism metal or carbon based?"

"Gee, I'm not quite sure. They have four arms, just like you, but I know they are not metal. But they were guiding the metal dragons. I know because I saw one myself. Those dragons, ho-ho," he laughed artificially, trying to be cute, "they aren't yours by any chance?"

"By no chance. They were bred by the vile Wankkers. I will tell you about them but first—I am being most forgetful. Those creatures we brought in with you. Are they Chingers by any chance? Or business associates?"

"They are human like me. My friends—or at least some of them are friends."

"Then we must see to their welfare for I am indeed being a bad host. I will get them in here—then I will tell you the loathsome story of the Wankkers."

CHAPTER 9

THE REST OF THE EXPEDITION WERE HERDED into the room by herding machines. They looked about suspiciously and fingered their blasters.

"It's okay—you're among friends," Bill called out quickly before there were any tragic accidents.

"You better amplify that statement," Praktis said. "Which friends are those exactly among all this ambulatory hardware?"

"The golden guy on the couch. Name of Zots and he seems to be in charge here."

"More than seems, friend Bill. I am Top Dog as you would say in your quaint language, though the definition of dog remains obscure. Do introduce me to your colleagues."

After Bill had done this, and they all had big drinks of water, Bill brought them up to date.

"It seems that Zots here, and all the rest of his gang, are metal-based life forms."

Praktis's eyes popped wide open when he heard this and a horde of scientific questions sprang to his lips. Bill saw them sticking there so he quickly went on. "He will fill you in on all that scientific stuff later, Admiral. But first he was about to tell us about the flying dragons that attacked us. They have something to do with something called Wankkers."

"A slight correction," Zots corrected. "They have been recently bred by the Wankkers. We keep a close eye on those metallic mothers because they are not to be trusted. Bill here has informed me that you war with the evil Chingers. You might say that our relationship with the Wankkers is very much the same. And, since they seem to have reared and trained the dragons for the Chingers, that would make us bedmates—would it not?"

"Allies is a better word," Praktis said.

"Point taken, dear friend. As to the Wankkers, they are out to destroy us so we must destroy them first."

"Just like humans and Chingers!" Bill said brightly.

"There would indeed appear to be a comparison. Here on Usa there are many and varied life forms—as you can see by looking about you. Millions of years ago life evolved in the warm pools of oil that adorn our landscape. Bathed by the rays of a benevolent sun, the process of evolution took many varied paths. Down through the ages there evolved the simple mineralvores who still graze the rich metal deposits in the hills and on the sandy prairies. But life is red, with rust, in tooth and fang. The machinevores evolved and preyed—and still prey—on the mineralvores. This is life as we know it and, I assume, as you know it?"

"Exactly!" Praktis agreed with great enthusiasm. "Parallel evolution. We must discuss this concept at great length..."

"As we shall. But first—the Wankkers. They evolved much as the other life forms did. But—how best to express it—they are insane in both the clinical and legal sense of the term. They are nuts. They have a screw loose. They have combined in a hideous alliance of mad machines and have been outcast by all sensible life forms. Long, long ago we sought to destroy them before they destroyed us. But just because they are insane it does not mean that they are stupid. The survivors of the metallic massacres fled and have built a stronghold in the mountains. Instead of living in peace they enslave others, beat and maltreat them. It is quite horrible. More horrible still to find them in league with these fleshly outcasts, the Chingers. Or so I am informed by friend Bill."

"True enough," Praktis said. "They directed the flying dragon attack."

"It makes sense. We have been aware of furious activity at the Wankker stronghold of late. Great numbers of the flying dragons have been observed by our spies flapping about the hills. We feared another attack, not realizing that these ravening hordes were directed against others. While happy for ourselves, we are desolated to hear of your misfortune."

"So are we," Praktis said. "I would dearly love to discuss evolution with you. But it will have to wait. Speaking from my military rank, not scientific, how do we get together for our mutual benefit? And the mutual destruction of our enemies."

"That *is* the question, isn't it? It will bear some thinking about. I would suggest that you now be shown to your quarters and take some light refreshments. A drop or two of lubricating oil, perhaps some powdered manganese? Oh, what am I saying!"

"Relax, Zots," Meta said. "We have our own food supplies with us. All we need is the stuff we were carrying—and a bare plot of ground."

"Simplicity itself and I have just so ordered. By radio signal of course. Relax and refresh yourselves and you will be summoned after I have conferred with my advisers."

"Seems like a nice place," Wurber said as they followed their wheeled guide through the riveted corridors. "Gosh we were lucky..."

"Shut up, you microcephalic moron," Praktis implied. "You drivel on without a drop of any intelligent thought ever troubling your clogged synapses. Don't you see the scientific wonders all about you? No, obviously not. But I do! I will write papers, publish books, be galaxy famous!"

"And get promoted in the navy too," Bill said sycophantically. "When you get all these machines fighting against the Chingers it will mean advances in your military career."

"The only promotion I want is back to civvy street and, yes, this might just do it."

"These are—your quarters—" their guide said in a very metallic voice, throwing open the door to a large room. It was barren of decorations or furnishings, other than the large hooks on the walls. Their bellboy indicated these with one of its tentacles. "You may hang yourselves from these hooks at night."

"Thanks a lot, Shiny," Meta sniffed. "But we have better ways to hang about at night. What about the patch of ground we asked for?"

"Provided. Walk this way please."

"If I walked that way I would need crutches."

She followed the machine through another door and out into a courtyard. "Looks great." She stamped on the bare soil, turned and called out. "Bring one of those melonsteak seeds. My stomach thinks my throat's been cut. Awwwrk!"

"Awwwrk? What does that suppose to mean?"

Praktis asked, turning towards the door just in time to see the sand boiling around her legs.

"Awwwrk!" he said himself. Then popped his eyes as she sank into the ground and vanished from sight.

"Help will be here soon," the guide machine said, extending an arm with an electronic eye on its tip to look into the hole.

It was right, too. The outer door burst open and Wurber was knocked to the floor by a torpedo-shaped machine that whizzed in on rows of little wheels. It nose-dived head first into the hole and vanished as quickly as Meta had done.

"What happened to Meta?" Bill asked, running into the courtyard.

"Beats me. The ground just opened up and she went down into it, zingo."

"I am getting reports now," Zots said as he entered the room. Still lounging on his gold lounger, now carried by six little carrying machines. "The tunnel is quite long and extends out under the outer wall. As far as the foothills. Ahh, yes. It emerges into a pleasant sunlit valley where your companion is being loaded onto a flying dragon. Our machine has been seen . . ."

Zots's throat was rasping and he took a quick slug of oil. "And that is it for the moment. The machine has been destroyed. I have dispatched warrior machines but I am afraid they are already too late. The lookouts report a dragon departing at great speed."

"Don't tell me—in the direction of the mountains," Praktis sneered. "Does your hospitality always include kidnapping?"

"I am mortified, dear guests, believe me. I am

so dishonored that if I had an electric drill handy I would commit seppuku. But perhaps my presence alive is better than dead for I shall organize pursuit and rescue. A combat machine is on the way here even as I speak. Might I suggest that one of your number accompany it to advise on matters fleshly in obtaining the freedom of the captive? Do we have a volunteer?"

There was a quick shuffle as they all moved back.

"I'm a garbage tug commander."

"I just got drafted, right off the farm."

"Electronics only—I never learned to shoot a gun."

"Rank, admiral. Occupation, scientist. Which leaves our only combat veteran."

All eyes were on Bill who chewed his lip worriedly and tried to figure a way out of this one.

"Congratulations, Third Lieutenant," Praktis said, stepping forward and clapping him on the shoulder. "Our hopes ride with you. To help you on your way—you will thank me next payday—I now commission you as a second lieutenant. And here is an extra charge for your blaster, should you need it. So—do not hesitate but go forth bravely. Because if you don't I'll shoot you between the eyes."

Bill saw the logic of this argument and stepped forward. There was a tremendous clanking as a squat, ugly and dangerous looking machine stamped into the room. It bristled with guns, spikes, grenade launchers, ray guns. It even had, horror of horrors!, a water hose sticking out where its bippy should be.

"A Mark I Fighting Devil," Zots said proudly. "It has been taught to talk your language and is at your disposal."

"I am at your disposal," it said in a gravelly voice. "Suggest reentry of chamber for all to avoid instant crushing."

It herded the puzzled humans inside—the machines had already zipped out of the way. The sky blackened and there was a great flapping as a silver ornithopter dropped into the courtyard. It hit the ground with a crash, sank low on its shock absorbers then bounced and swayed to rest. A folding ladder rattled down its side.

Bill looked at it with deep suspicion. "I don't believe it," he muttered. "Birds fly by flapping their wings. Machines can't. They are too heavy to fly by flapping."

"You have just got to believe your eyes," Zots said. "It is an aluminum-based lifeform, not iron. In any case—good luck, newfound companion Bill. Such a brave fleshling sallying forth and soon to face death seeking a comrade. Defend him well, Fighting Devil."

"To the final erg of energy, the last drop of lube oil," it rasped.

When Bill hesitated it kindly lifted him onto the ladder and clambered up behind him.

Feeling more than slightly put-upon, Bill climbed into the saddle on the ornithopter's back and slipped his feet into the stirrups. Behind him Mark I bolted himself into place. Zots called up to him.

"May the weak nuclear force and the strong nuclear force be with you."

Their metallic mount buzzed and the four wings rose slowly, then began to beat, faster and faster. The thing vibrated like crazy and when it seemed like it would shake itself to pieces it finally stirred and lifted from the ground. Bill held on for dear life and clamped his jaw shut so his teeth would not be crashed together and splintered from his head.

"This is terrible!" he gritted.

"If you know a better way to fly—tell me about it," the Fighting Devil said with total machine indifference. "Now, if you look ahead you will see the peaks of the mountain range of Prtzlkzxyñdlp-69 coming into view now. In your language Prtzlkzxyñdlp-69 might be translated as mountains where hope is lost, despair triumphs and it snows all summer..."

"Listen, Mark, I could do without the travelogue. Have you heard anything more about what is happening?"

"But of course. I am in constant radio communication with base. Our spies report that the dragon has landed and your companion has vanished from sight. A combat squad has been sent out to destroy their observation posts. That mission has now been accomplished, with great losses of course, but no sacrifice is too great for our new comrades in arms. Now we will be able to land, without being seen, very close to the enemy. Hold tight—we're going down!"

It wasn't the going down that bothered Bill. In fact it was kind of fun, a little like one of those rides in an amusement park. It was when they leveled out and flew up the valley that the hair stood up on his neck. The machine fluttered and flapped along, bouncing off the rock walls, slithering down the slopes, then staggering on. With a last crunching impact that bent one of its wings in half, it side-slipped into a cul-de-sac and crashed-landed among the rocks. It lay there steaming, one wing bent up into the air. With shaking hands Bill climbed down to the welcome ground.

"Thanks for a great ride," he muttered, sarcasm dripping from his lips.

"Oh, thank you," the ornithopter said in a high, squeaky voice. Its eyes creaked as it rotated in its socket to look down at him. "I regret that I have but one life to give to my comrades—and new, wet friends..." Its voice croaked into silence, the eye dulled and closed.

"It was a far better thing it did than it had ever done..." the combat machine intoned.

"All right, I know the rest of the quote. What next?"

"We penetrate the enemy stronghold."

"We do, do we? Just like that. Has it ever been done before?"

"No. But the Mark I Fighting Devil has never seen action on this front before."

"Great. If your fighting skills are as impressive as your ego we can't lose."

"We can't. This plan has been developed by CBTATC, the Central Brain Trust and Tactics Committee. It goes like this. Their observation posts have been wiped out so an attack can be made unobserved. And here come the attackers now."

It pulled Bill aside an instant before the wheeled, tracked, and legged battle machines swept by. Bristling with weapons, rugged and formidable, the ground shook as they advanced. They sang too, a battle song, that Bill could not understand, which was probably just as well. As soon as they had passed, Bill and Mark I hurried in their wake. The canyon they followed twisted and turned—and gave an occasional glimpse of the Wankker citadel up ahead. Then the distant singing ended in a mighty explosion and clash of metal against metal.

"Battle has been joined," Mark said. "The defenders have emerged to beat off the attackers. We must hurry for this attack is fated to fail. Here we are."

The battle machine ran up to the rocky wall of the canyon, apparently no different from the rest of the rock. But very different it proved when Mark I poked a metal finger into a crevice and a slab of rock swung out like a door to disclose a dark opening. Before Bill could protest he was pushed inside and the rock swung shut again. There was just enough room for them to stand. And look out because, by some application of alien science the rock, so solid looking from the outside, was transparent from inside.

Once more the ground shook under the metallic tread of the attacking army. Except this time it was the retreating army. Their diminished numbers swept by outside—pursued closely by an equally obnoxious herd of enemy fighting machines. Shells whistled and exploded, lightning bolts flashed. Then the attackers hurtled out of sight, though many of their gallant fighters lay dismembered and smoking in their wake. The defenders crunched over and around the casualties and disappeared in hot pursuit.

"What now?" Bill asked.

"Wait. It is almost time."

The camp followers began to appear and trundled by in the wake of the victorious army. Ammunition carriers, tankers and battery rechargers. And salvage carriers. The last of these rumbled by outside, then stopped to extend a long arm and lift a dismembered warrior aboard. Dropping it with a clang on others of its kind in the large hopper at the rear. By the time it started forward again all of its combat comrades had carried the counterattack around the bend and out of sight.

The Fighting Devil opened the rock door a crack, extended an insulated arm—and shot a lightning bolt into the vehicle outside. It crackled with surging volts, shuddered and died.

"Its central control circuits are cooked," Mark I said with metallic pleasure. "Otherwise it is perfectly functional. We must quickly board and hide under the wreckage. Now!"

They scuttled out and Mark I pushed aside some junk, then dropped it behind them. Enough light filtered down for Bill to see a flexible rod slip out of its armpit and drill into the machine. A moment later the salvage carrier quivered, then hummed to life. Spun on its treads and started back in the direction from whence it had come.

Bill was not happy, not happy at all.

CHAPTER **10**

"WE MUST CEASE CONVERSATION WHEN WE approach the wall," Mark I said. "This creature had a mighty small brain and it will take all of my concentration to act extremely stupid when the entrance guardians contact me. We approach."

Tension very quickly gave way to boredom since Bill hadn't the slightest idea what was happening. They moved, slowed, stopped, went on. The light that trickled down dimmed, then brightened again.

"What's going on?" he whispered.

"We are safely inside the enemy's fortress. Would you like to see what is happening?"

"That would be great."

A panel opened in the machine's side and a flat TV screen slid out and lit up. On the screen a roughly finished tunnel streamed by. Then it opened out into a stone-walled chamber that was being enlarged by small, pick-bearing machines. To encourage them in their labors a whip machine, bristling with barbed wire flails, rumbled along behind them whipping as it went. The clash of wire on bare metal elicited metallic moans of pain.

"Robot slaves," Mark I intoned grimly. "What agonies they suffer. How evil the Wankkers are.

They must be wiped out, destroyed down to the last nut and bolt."

There were more corridors, but nothing else was to be seen anywhere as interesting as the robot slaves. And Bill was beginning to get carsick, what with the motion, dust, spilled oil and everything. He fought hard not to flip his cookies. Then they stopped—and the floor dropped out from under him and Bill almost lost the regurgitant battle. An instant later he forgot his sickness as the cargo shifted and began to fall in on them. Only a rapid extension of one of Mark I's arms saved him from being crushed.

"As you can see, we're in the elevator," the machine rasped. "On the way down to the flying dragon nursery."

"The *what?* How do you know? You've never been here before."

"I asked the way. No one suspects a machine as stupid as this one. Quiet—we arrive!"

After what appeared to be an infinity of rumblings and clankings, and more stone corridors, they lurched to a stop. The load of junk creaked and more light filtered down. Mark I rattled to life and spoke.

"Mission accomplished. We have penetrated the Wankker stronghold and have descended to the lair of the flying dragons. Here is where they are born and live. And eat. They eat junk, of course. They breathe out flame to melt it. I am unloading in their storage chamber. Now, I lift this piece—move quickly to safety!"

Bill clambered free of the shifting debris and jumped to the stone floor of the immense chamber. Mark I was right behind him—with the flexible cable still running to the controls of the carrier. Under his guidance the thing lurched forward and a projecting corner cut into a power cable. Electricity sizzled and spat and it once more slumped into silence. Mark I had disconnected in time and trotted over to join Bill.

"They will find its brain sizzled and will suspect nothing. Our presence here is unknown. We will now rescue your comrade."

"You know where she is?"

"I have strong suspicions. I have determined the location of the Chingers who undoubtedly arranged its abduction. If we find them, we find it."

"Her; girls are called her, not it. Sounds wonderful," Bill said through suddenly chattering teeth. "But let us see if we can find her without finding them."

They skulked through dark corridors and crept past open doorways. Deeper and ever deeper into the enemy lair.

"They are all around us," Mark I whispered, drawing Bill into a dark alcove. "I'll send out some spy-bugs."

A door opened in its chest and tiny dark forms, like metal cockroaches, scuttled down his legs and vanished in the dusk.

"Reports coming in. Roomful of soft green creatures, four arms, doing indescribable things."

"Chingers!"

"The spy-bug is moving on. Dragon in here . . . oops. That one got stepped on. Next one reporting in. A room with a barred and locked door. The spy-bug is through the bars. Lights glaring on the form of your companion chained to the wall."

"The fiends are torturing her!"

"I wouldn't know about that. But she is unmoving. Asleep or dead."

"Let's go!"

They went. Walking in silent apprehension.

Which is all right as long as you wipe your shoes off afterwards.

"That is the door. Instead of blowing it down I will use a silent lockpick to open it."

"Yes, great, do it!"

There was a small metallic click and the door swung wide. They hurried through and Mark I closed and sealed it behind them. Bill gasped as he saw the silent figure, slumped, hanging from the chains.

"She's dead!" Bill groaned.

"No I'm not," Meta said, opening her eyes and yawning. "But I'm damned uncomfortable. I'm very glad to see you, Bill darling. Can you do something about these chains?"

Even as she spoke the Fighting Devil had scuttled to her side and with rapid snips of a cable cutter had set her free.

"Meta, this is Mark I Fighting Devil."

"A pleasure to meet you, Mark. Thanks for leading my shipmate here. And what plans do you have for the future?"

"A diversion has been arranged, a different escape route opened up. But, hist, wait a moment— I sense movement in the ceiling!"

It moved over, looked up—and was struck by an orange bolt of lightning that flared down from above. The Fighting Devil glowed all over and rattled in every joint. Smoke began oozing out of its vents. Then it slumped down, silent and motionless. The Fighting Devil had fought its last fight.

A tiny door opened in the far wall and a Chinger stepped through. Bill grabbed out his blaster.

"Don't try it, Bill. Gee—it would be suicide. There are a hundred guns trained on you." To prove his words more tiny doors opened and gun-toting Chingers pointed their muzzles out at him. And the muzzles of their guns as well.

"Put it down, slow and careful, and no one will get hurt."

"Do it, Bill," Meta said. "You got no choice. I'm sorry I got you into this mess."

He hesitated, wanting to go down fighting. Wanting to stay alive as well. But he who hesitates is lost he discovered when the nearest Chinger jumped into the air and grabbed the blaster, then tossed it to one of his companions. And one of his fingernails as well. He sucked at the finger and felt sorry for himself.

"Gee—" the Chinger said. "Now we can relax and sit back and talk, just like old times. Right, Bill."

"Your voice is familiar. . . ." He gaped. "But how could it be. I don't know any Chingers. Or maybe just one of them—but he's dead. Eager Beager!"

"Gee—that's me, in the green flesh, old buddy."

"You can't be! I saw you eaten by a giant snake on Veniola, the fog-shrouded planet that creeps in orbit around the ghoulish green star Hernia—"

"Spare me the details, I've been there. If your memory had not been destroyed by years of alcohol and military service, you would have remembered that we Chingers come from a dense, heavy planet. I just gave the snake indigestion, opened its jaw, and even broke a tooth off it getting out."

Meta was sidling away, looking from one to the other of them, shock and horror on her features.

"Bill—you know a Chinger! You must be a spy. . ."

"Gee—you better relax, lady. It's a long story so I'll shorten it. Many years ago when our mutual friend was a recruit I was one too. A spy. Bill discovered this and turned me in."

"You couldn't be a spy! You would be recognized."

"A keen observation. I was inside a dummy human robot which the other dummies never noticed. And I have been meaning to ask, Bill, gee—how *did* you find out about me?"

"Your camera-watch went click." Bill figured that after all the time that had passed, telling the Chinger now wouldn't matter. And it might help to at least appear to cooperate.

"Gee—I thought it might be that. The new model spy-watch doesn't click, you will be cheered to know. Now, to pick up where we left off that hot, humid day so long ago. In our talk you said that your race, homo sapiens, *likes* war. Do you still believe that?"

"Yes. Only more so."

"And you, dear lady, member of the gentler sex in uniform. Why do you fight this war?"

"Because I was drafted."

"Agreed. But if you were not drafted—would you have enlisted?"

"Maybe. To make the galaxy safe for humans. After all, you filthy Chingers started this war and want to kill and eat us all."

"The last is a physical impossibility—our metabolisms are too different. But the truth is that we are a peaceful race and loathe violence. It is really you humans who make war on us."

"Do you expect me to believe that old bushwah?" she sniffed.

"Believe it," Bill said. "It's true. The whole war

is a fake to keep the military in power and the factory wheels turning."

"Gee—the same can be said of all wars down through human history. I have become a keen student of humanity since I saw you last, Bill. So—gee—would you help me, both of you?"

"Death to Chingers," Meta muttered.

"Help you do what?"

"End the war, of course. You *would* like that, wouldn't you?"

"I'm sort of used to the job now—"

"Gee—Bill—you are being a dummy! I don't mean you personally. I mean your entire society. Wouldn't it be nice to free your fellow men, and women, from the burden of warfare once and for all? End all the death, mutilation and destruction. How about that?"

"You would put a lot of people out of work."

"I can't believe that I'm hearing this. What about you, Meta? You look like a sensible girl. Do you really believe that unending war is the only future for mankind?"

"I never really thought about it. But we really have to protect ourselves."

"Against what—whom, or which? Let me tell you about recent history—because I was involved in it myself. Settle down on the nice stone floor and listen."

The Chinger leaned back comfortably on his tail, tucked his thumbs into his marsupial pouch, and told them—

THE CHINGER'S TALE

My youth was spent in happy study at the university, whose name you could not pronounce, on the Chinger home planet, which you will never find. In those halcyon days of yore, BH, Before Humans, life was an idyllic pleasure. I graduated head of my class and my family was so proud. They held a grand party and all my siblings came, pouch–brothers we call them. All males of course, for ours was a male family. There are female families, neuter families and *stupidaggine* families—but I digress. This is not the time to talk about sex.

After the banquet of grilled snake's legs, my mouth waters at the memory, my old teacher took me aside—may his aged gray scales be ever blessed!—and asked me what I intended to do with my life. I told him I had considered teaching, but he cozened me against it. "Get out into the world, young lizard," he said. "Or better the worlds." And he was right. I opened my first exopology text and I knew that this was what I wanted to devote my life to. The study of alien life forms. I got a doctorate for my paper on Veniolan swamp denizens and went on for my masters in Caca-bene dung roller beetles. Life was indeed sweet. It was then we had our first contact with homo sapiens.

This was to be my specialty, I felt it in my bones. We had a small settlement on the planet Ca-cabene, built around a heavy-metal mine. I knew it well from my years of study in the surrounding swamps. When the FTL message was received that a strange spaceship had been detected landing on the planet I hurried to the town hall just as fast as I could swim. I volunteered to lead the exopological contact team—and I was selected. Stopping only long enough to pack my Easilearner Machine Translator, often abbreviated to EMT, I grabbed the first spacer going in the right direction.

I had a good team, highly skilled and eager

Chingers. No contact had been made with the space travelers. The locals were awaiting our arrival, but they were being kept under close scrutiny. We joined the observation team in their jungle camp. It was then that I had my first intimation that these aliens were different from all other life forms ever contacted before.

"Bgr," the head observer said, "these aliens are something else again." He called me Bgr because that is my name, or why I adapted the nom de guerre Eager Beager that you know me by. But I digress. I was warned to be very careful with my first contact since the aliens had, up to that moment, killed eighty-one thousand creatures from forty different species. Most interesting, since exopologists only work with live specimens and save dissection for those which die of natural causes. This was death on a massive scale and I was thrilled at the novelty of this new species to study.

Having been warned, I approached the alien encampment with extreme caution, swimming underwater through the swamp with my EMT sealed in a plastic bag. When I was close enough to hear voices I planted the EMT, turned it on and split. I retrieved the recordings the following night and discovered that the machine had worked perfectly. Much conversation had been recorded. There was a growing vocabulary list and a preliminary linguistic analysis. I memorized everything, chuckling at witticisms like "blow it out your barracks bag" and "your mother wears GI shoes." Within a fortnight the EMT had done its job and I felt prepared to carry on a coherent conversation with the space travelers. The next morning I eagerly awaited sunrise outside the electric barrier that ringed the encampment. When they emerged I addressed them.

"Greetings, O strangers who have crossed the trackless wastes of space, greetings."

I then ducked back behind the trunk of a large tree as the expected bullets, shells and blaster blasts blasted all around me. When the firing had died down I tried again.

"I come in peace. I am unarmed. I am the representative of an intelligent race who anticipates friendly contact with another intelligent race."

There was less firing this time. When I repeated the aims of my friendly mission in greater detail, a few more times, the firing finally stopped and a voice called out to me.

"Come out with your hands in the air—and don't try anything funny."

"I cannot raise my hands into the air, since I have none, but I will raise my paws instead. All four of them since I have four arms. Hold your fire, dear friends from space, for here I come."

As you can imagine it was a traumatic moment, for me if not for them, for there could have been a trigger-happy microcephalic who might blast me. But science is not without risks! But opposed to my personal safety was this opportunity to be part of the first contact between intelligent races. I stepped out proudly—and dropped flat as a bullet whistled by.

"Take that trigger-happy microcephalic's gun away!" a voice shouted. "Okay, lizzy, you're safe now."

Arms high I stepped forward proudly and, as they say, the rest is history. When they saw how small I was curiosity replaced fear, for give mankind that, yours is a curious and intelligent race. They all got their cam-

eras out and took pictures, then the leader wanted
pictures of him and me shaking hands. Which we did,
though unhappily I squeezed too hard and broke three
of his fingers. I was most apologetic, explained about
being from a 10G planet and all, and he forgave me as
they bandaged him up.

After that it was clear sailing for quite a while. We
invited them to our settlement and showed them our
technology and such. They took plenty of notes and
pictures, but gave us very little in return other than
diagrams of electric eggbeaters, power operated shoe-
horns, pencil sharpeners and such. Everything else
was what they called a military secret. Since both
terms were new to us we were very interested as you
can imagine. Soon after this they invited us to appoint
a delegation to return with them to their home world.
We were thrilled at this, I more than ever when I was
officially appointed as ambassador. I selected a staff
and we joined them in their spacer. By this time we
knew that our metabolisms were completely different
so, in addition to our communication and recording
equipment, we packed a considerable supply of dehy-
drated beetles and other rations.

What a wonderful experience! We discovered that
once the trip had begun they were more outgoing.
They answered all our questions, even the most technical ones, and were grateful when our physicist
pointed out ways of improving their FTL communication equipment. I was in fourteenth heaven as I made
the notes for my book, the first exopological text to be
written about homo sapiens. The commander of the
spacer, a Captain Queeg, offered to help me in any
way he could. I decided an interview in depth should
begin at once. Armed with a recorder, notebook and
stylobiro I went to his quarters.

"This is pleasure of greatest importance, Captain Queeg," I told him. "I know scarcely how to begin."

"Why not start by calling me Charley, which is my first name. And you?"

"We have but one name and mine is Bgr."

"Bugger?"

"Beager is closer. Two words you have often used intrigue me. What is a secret?"

"Something you don't tell anyone. You keep it secret."

"If a fact is kept secret then how can communication and learning be accomplished?"

"Easily—on other matters. But secrets are kept secret."

My stylobiro flew across my pad. "Fascinating. Now the other word, often linked with 'secret'. Military."

He frowned. "Why do you want to know this?"

"Why? Why not. Many things we asked about we were told were military secrets. Both concepts are unknown to us."

"You don't keep secrets?"

"We see no reason to. Knowledge is public and meant to be shared by all."

"But you got armies and navies don't you?"

Oh how my stylobiro flew. "Negative, negative. Meaning of terms unknown."

"Let me explain then. Armies and navies are large groups of people with weapons who defend those nearest and dearest against the vicious enemy."

"But what is *enemy*," I asked, getting into deeper water all the time.

"Enemies are other groups, countries, people

who want to take your country, land, freedom away. And kill you."

"But who would want to do that?"

"The enemy," he said grimly.

I was at a loss for words, a rare thing for a Chinger of education. I finally managed to control my spinning thoughts and speak. "But we have no enemies. All Chingers of course live in peace with other Chingers, since to consider injuring another means that another could consider injuring you and that is nonviable. And, in our voyages to other worlds, we have never met an intelligent species before. We study the species we meet, aid them if we can, but have found no enemies so far." At that point a sudden thought devastated me and I could barely speak, barely choke out the words. "You humans, you are not our enemies are you?"

"Of course not," he laughed loudly at the idea. "We like you little green guys, really we do."

"And of course we are not your enemies," I assured him. "We could not be since, until this moment, the term was unknown to us."

I decided to let this strange and discomfiting matter rest there and went on to other topics of interest. When I returned and told my associates about *military* and *secrets,* then about *enemies* they were just as baffled as I was. These alien concepts of the aliens were really alien. It was our physician who suggested the idea that there might be a disease that infected mankind, a form of mental illness that made them see enemies where none existed. This was a concept we could deal with. It even cheered us because, if this concept were true, we might help them find a cure for the disease. It was in this enthusiastic mood that we landed on the human planet named Spiovente.

This may sound incredibly naive to a sophisticated audience, but it is true. We were dealing with concepts the mind cannot stomach, so were suffering from mental gastric upsets. However our studies terminated rather unexpectedly. One of our number proved to be *krndl*. This is a term of a sexual nature, having to with our unique physical structure, and too complex to explain. But it does require that the Chinger so affected must return to our world, our society, within a limited period of time. When this was explained to our hosts they grew agitated and withdrew.

My companions were not disturbed by this. I was. I was beginning to assemble a mental operating pattern for homo sapiens—and I did not like it. These were just suspicions at the time and I failed to acquaint the others of my thoughts since they were so outrageous. In fact there was little time to do this since at that moment we were summoned to the meeting hall on the third story of the building where our studies were taking place. Captain Queeg was the only human present and he appeared to be upset.

"What has gotta be, has gotta be," he said cryptically. "I'm sorry."

"Sorry for what?" I asked.

"Just sorry. I really do like you little green fellers, I really do . . ."

When he said this I knew that my worst fears had become reality. I called out to my companions to flee at once, but they were too shocked to understand. So I alone survived. I hurled myself through the window as the doors opened and the firing began.

It was obvious by hindsight that when we had agreed to accompany the humans we would never be allowed to return. We had been told secrets, and a number of them of a military nature, which would have to be kept secret. And there was only one sure way of doing that. Kill us all.

I brooded over this and sorrowed for my dead companions. And looked for a way to get off this planet and warn my fellow Chingers. It was very difficult since all spacecraft were undergoing intense and complete inspection before being allowed to leave. That was when I conceived the notion of human disguise. My first altered robot was not as sophisticated as the later Eager Beager persona, but it sufficed to get by in a crowd on a rainy night. The crowd happened to be a group of draftees off to the wars and they were so wrapped up in their own troubles that they never noticed my rather unusual appearance.

The war began after that. Once in space I entered the communications room by walking through the steel wall, coming from a 10G world does have its advantages, and sent an FTL message of warning. It was believed, since by that time humans had been attacking our establishments wherever they could be found. It takes two to make a war work. We had to either knuckle under or fight back.

The reluctant choice was made.

CHAPTER 11

"ARE WE SUPPOSED TO BELIEVE THAT?" META sneered.

"It is but the truth."

"I don't think that you little four-armed bastards can even spell the truth!"

"Tea, arr, you, tea, haich."

"Don't get smart with me, buddy. I'm supposed to believe that holier-than-thou bowb? Your bunch is honest, truthful, upright. While we humans are lying warmongers."

"That is your interpretation, not mine. Though I find it quite descriptive and will make a note of it. I did not say that we Chingers are models of perfection. We are not. But we do not lie and we do not start wars."

"You lied to me," Bill said. "When you were a spy."

"Correction humbly accepted. Until we met you humans we did not lie. Now, naturally, we do. As one of the exigencies of total warfare. But we still do not start wars."

"A likely story," Meta sniffed. "You expect me to believe that if we stopped the war tomorrow that you would just go away like that?"

"Of a certainty."

"You wouldn't maybe attack suddenly when we

weren't looking, a preemptive strike? Get us before we got you."

"I assure you that we would not. This concept, which you accept so willingly, is alien to us. We fight, when forced to for our own survival, in defense. We are incapable of fighting an offensive war."

"War is war," Bill said, making what he thought was an intelligent remark.

"It certainly is not," Beager said with some heat. "War is about power. It exists only for its own sake. The object of power is power. You remember our military training, Bill, when we were draftees together? Power is tearing the human mind to pieces and putting the pieces together again in new shapes of your own choosing."

"Enough theory," Meta said. "What's going to happen to us?"

"I want to enlist your help, as I told you earlier. I would like you to help me end this war."

"Why?" Bill asked.

The Chinger jumped up and down in rage and stamped holes in the stone floor. "Why? Haven't you heard a bowbing word that I said?"

"Don't lose your cool, kid," Meta cozened. "Bill's a good guy, but too many years in the military have numbed his mind. I know what you are saying. You want to brainwash us to agree with you, so we then go back and stop the war so you can secretly attack and kill us all. Right?"

The Chinger stepped back, aghast, looked from one to the other, wrung all four of its paws together in disbelief. "And you pass yourselves off as an intelligent species? I don't know what to do with you!"

"Let us go," Bill said with immense practicality.

"Not until you see some bit of reason. If I cannot

sow even the slightest seed of doubt in your resisting minds—what chance do we have with the rest of your race? Is this war destined to go on for eternity?"

"If the military have their way, it will," Bill said and Meta nodded agreement.

"I need a drink of water," Beager said, "or something stronger."

He staggered back through the little door. As soon as it had closed behind him, Bill and Meta turned and ran towards the tunnel out of the room. Although Beager the Chinger had been upset he had not lost all of his marbles. A steel gate fell down from the ceiling with an immense crash and sealed the exit.

"We are trapped, lost, forgotten, good as dead," Bill suggested.

Meta nodded reluctant agreement. "That about sums it up."

"Do not despair," a metallic voice said and they turned about to see the Mark I Fighting Devil begin to stir and twitch.

"You're alive!" Bill said. "But you were electrocuted, fried dead."

"That's what they were supposed to think. But you don't knock out a Fighting Devil that easily. My brain is sealed in a lead box where my tushie should be. The head is just for show. I just let them think that they had sizzled me. Hoping they would forget about me, which they have. So I waited for an opportune moment—"

"Which is now!"

"Right the first time. This way to the dragon pens—where we put the plan into action."

"Which plan?"

"The plan I worked out while listening to that sickening pacifist drivel. If there were no war there would be no place for Fighting Devils. What would I do if peace broke out? End up rusting away in some free oil kitchen with the rest of the out-of-work machines. Roll on the war! This way."

It plunged into the mouth of the nearest tunnel while Bill and Meta trotted expectantly after. There was a metal grille here as well—which crashed open after being hit by a well-aimed zap of energy. "Now let's move it before the greenies catch wise."

Mark I speeded up then and the two humans had to run to keep pace, panting and staggering. Sweat soon beaded their foreheads, ran down into their eyes and blinded them. So much so that when the Fighting Devil suddenly stopped they ran right into it.

"Wait here out of sight," Mark I commanded. "While I arrange some transportation."

Then it poked its head into the nearest doorway.

"Any dragons about? Ohh, I see—hi guys. Can I have a volunteer to light a fire for me? You there, big boy, you look like hot stuff."

A wave of greasy flame washed over the Fighting Devil who nodded happily. "That will do fine. Would you come this way. Thank you."

Mark I came back into the corridor followed by the shining, winged length of the dragon. The Fighting Devil let it writhe by, then closed the door.

"Where's the fire?" the dragon asked. "Say— aren't those human beans, the ones we are fighting?"

"They sure are!"

"Want me to fry them?" It inhaled rapidly and stoked its flame; its eyes glowed with pyromaniacal zeal.

"Not really. What I want you to do is feel the gun barrel in your left ear. Got it? Just nod. Good. So now you will do as I say or I blow the whole head away. Agreed?"

"Yeah, yeah. But what's this all about?"

"You just changed sides. You are going to fly the three of us out of here and over to my mob where you will be amply rewarded. OK?"

"You're on. The latrine rumor has it that there were no survivors from the last raid the Chingers arranged. So you got a willing convert. Climb aboard. We'll go out the back passage—no one uses it this time of day."

Mark I climbed to the dragon's back first and perched on the row of spines there. Only when it had drilled some holes and bolted itself into place did it call down to the others.

"Here we go. It is going to be a rough ride so I will hold you in my unbreakable metal embrace."

Someone—or something—shouted hoarsely from back in the corridor and a projectile of some kind whizzed over the dragon and exploded against the wall. Bill and Meta broke the interstellar dragon-back-climbing record by many seconds. The creature lurched off even as they did. With microseconds to spare Mark I clutched onto them as the dragon slid down a greasy slope and out into space. Then flapped off.

"I've radioed ahead," Mark I shouted over the rush of wind, "so we get the right kind of reception. This has sure been a busy day."

It got busier. Their escape had not gone unnoticed. In fact it had been very noticed and the alarm was out. Sheets of flame sheeted after them, waves of forcefields waved undulously. The dragon closed its wings and dropped like a rock. The air above them crackled and smoked with lambent energies, so close

that their heads began to cook and Meta's hair started
to smoke. Then they were out of range in the valley
and all they had to worry about was crashing to death
on the stony floor rushing up towards them. No, that
wasn't all that they had to worry about. Heatseeking,
radar operated, and sonar orientated missiles were
hurtling in their direction. But the Fighting Devil was
really a fighting devil and more than a match for this
new assault. The chill blast of a coldray diverted the
heatseeking warheads, while a radar canceler canceled
the radar. This left the sonar detectors which were not
so easily misled. But Mark I was up to this challenge as
well. Its thorax opened and an amplified loudspeaker
popped out and emitted an immense blast of sound
like a colossal fart. The remaining missiles tumbled
end over end and crashed to the valley below. The
dragon and the dragon riders almost crashed as well—
but the flapping furnace extended its wings at the last
moment and pulled out of the dive with an 11G turn. Its
toenails scratched sparks from the rocks, so close to the
ground were they.

Now it flew energetically down the valley while
Mark I hummed a bloodthirsty war song and its two
human riders tried to recover from the frying,
crushing and deafening.

"We got company," the Fighting Devil said,
pointing to their rear. The dragon poked out an eye
and swiveled it backwards and sniffed.

"That's only a flock of flying dragons," it
sniffed contemptuously and belched a cloud of
smoke as it cleared its throat.

Bill coughed out a lungful of smoke and looked
back red-eyed at the sky filled with attacking
dragons.

"They'll get us! Cook us to death!"

The dragon belched again. "No way. They're all my nestmates, egg-buddies from the same brood. They can't fly worth bowb. All the real flyers were lost in the Chinger raid."

"If you're so great why weren't you wiped out with them?"

"I didn't go on the mission. I was out sick that day with heartburn."

"Can you also outfly those other dragons coming along the valley from up ahead?"

Their noble metal steed took one look and dived into a narrow side-valley.

"No way. That's the Dawn Patrol returning from a raid. They've got afterburners. Hold on—I'll try and lose them in this maze of intersecting valleys."

They hung on—and Bill closed his eyes and moaned. The dragon hurtled under overhanging ledges, screamed in tight turns and almost splashed into an oil lake. It was panting like a steam engine now as they hurtled out of the last valley and were in the open over a vast plain.

"Running out of . . . fuel . . ." it gasped and exhaled just a trace of coalgas.

Mark I extended an electron telescope and looked to the rear, then swiveled it to gaze down at the ground below. "We're OK," it said. "You cut them off at the pass. Land there, three points off your starboard bow. There is an oil spring bubbling up through the coal beds."

"Yummy . . ." the dragon croaked. "I really need . . . a fix."

It wasn't much of a landing. The dragon came in nose first and plowed into the ground, cartwheeling end over end. But Mark I had nerves of steel and held on until the last instant—then dived free carrying his human charges with him. It did a couple of nifty shoulder rolls and came up standing on its feet.

"You—can let go now—" Meta said, struggling in its steel embrace.

"Quite right, sorry."

Bill dropped to the ground, rolled over and was instantly sick.

"Clean it up when you're through," Meta said with great sensitivity. "Where are we now?"

"Haven't a clue," Mark I said, spinning its telescope in all directions. "I lost orientation with all those turns. Not that it matters—since we seem to have shaken off our pursuers. Let's stoke up this drooping dragon and then I'll see if I can locate a radio beacon."

The Fighting Devil, still in fine form, trotted over to the nearest outcropping of coal and blasted it with an explosive round of cannon fire. When the dust had settled it filled its arms with broken chunks and brought them back. The dragon lay flat and unmoving, its neck extended along the ground. Its eyes were closed and only the slightest trickle of smoke came from its nostrils.

"Pry its jaw open and I'll push these in," Mark I said.

Bill hauled on one side and Meta on the other and, after great effort, the jaw creaked open. Mark I shoved in the coal, pushing it down as far as he could, then leaned into the dragon's mouth and shot a bolt of lightning down its throat. When the coal was crackling nicely it pulled its head out and slammed the jaw shut. Very shortly thereafter smoke began to trickle out between the dragon's teeth. It moaned and shuddered and breathed deep.

"Just got it in time," Fighting Devil said smugly, very proud of itself.

"Wonderful," Bill agreed. "So whenever you are through patting yourself on the back, you might find a high spot and tune in on those beacons you mentioned."

They sat, exhausted, on a small orange sand dune while Mark I climbed a spire of nearby rock. Meta recovered first and put her arm around Bill and gave a tender squeeze.

"Isn't it romantic with the green sunrise, this orange dune . . ."

"And this red-hot dragon dying at our feet. Come on, Engine Mate First Class, you know better than to associate with an officer."

"It's more of an offense to be immune to the attractions of a lovely woman. Here, look at these."

She pulled down the zipper at the neck of her uniform, ever so slowly, so that pink magnificence swelled into view. Bill, now glowing with lust as redly as the dragon, leaned forward, hands extended, just as the Fighting Devil reappeared.

"What an interesting mating ritual. Do continue, I find it fascinating."

"Metallic peeping-tom," Meta sniffed as she stood up and rezipped. "Why aren't you out there looking for radio beacons?"

"Because I have found one. Very weak, off in that direction. We must be in the Badlands, an unexplored area of volcanic emissions, earthquakes, landslides and quicksand."

"Charming. So let's revive sleeping beauty here and flap off."

The dragon stirred feebly at her words and croaked, "Oil . . ."

"Help is on the way," Mark I said as it scurried off to the nearest pool, where it extended a tube and sucked a quantity into some interior tank. The dragon feebly opened its jaw when it returned and the Fighting Devil pumped the lot down its throat. There was the muffled whump of an interior explosion and flame jetted from the creature's nostrils.

"That's better," it said, sitting up and hiccuping little bursts of smoke. "Keep the home fires burning, I always say. What's next?"

"We fly thataway," Mark I said, pointing. "As soon as you are up to it."

"Won't be long. This stuff tastes like prime anthracite and 30–60 oil. Be right back."

The dragon lumbered to the outcropping and noshed great mouthfuls of coal, washing them down with deep swigs of oil. Very quickly the outcropping was cropped and the pool drunk dry. It flapped its wings to test them and breathed out a long tongue of flame.

"All systems go, boiler pressure up and I'm as hot as a Spanish pistol. And just as horny. It's a good thing there aren't any dragonettes here. Though you are kind of cute there, rusty!"

Mark I rolled backwards with alacrity, all its weapons raised. "None of that kinky interspecies sex, you overheated flying machine! We Fighting Devils reproduce by vegetative propagation in any case—so knock it off."

The dragon miffedly belched flame and reluctantly ordered them to board. Its skin was almost too hot to touch, but cooled down as soon as they were airborne. Filled to bursting with overheated orgone it flapped into high gear and tore towards the horizon.

"What's that ahead," Bill asked, blinking into the slipstream.

"Beats me, mate," Mark I shrugged. "Never been here before. But it appears to be an immense plateau rising from the desert below."

As they grew close they saw that the mysterious object was an immense plateau rising from the desert below. The dragon soared on the updraft near the cliff and circled to gain altitude. As they passed over the edge they saw that the plateau was covered in mysterious green growth.

"Doesn't look good," Mark I said.

"Not good at all!" the dragon screeched, then groaned in pain as projectiles roared up from the plateau below, impacting and exploding on its hide.

"I'm hit!" it cried as its portside wing was blown off. "We're going down!"

CHAPTER 12

"IS THIS THE END?" BILL CROAKED AS THE
green ground rushed up towards them.

"Fighting Devils die laughing—with a song on
their loudspeakers! Yo-ho Tee-tee Ho-Ho!"

"Kiss me, hearty, Bill!"

With an incredible crunching and snapping the
dragon crashed into the jungle, because that was
what the green stuff was. Great boughs broke under
its weight, thick vines stretched and snapped. Down
and down, slower and slower it fell through the verdant vegetation that gave way, bit by bit, and slowed
their descent. Until, with one last snap of one last
giant liana, they dropped softly into the field of tall
grass below.

"That was nice," Meta said, stepping gently
down from the dragon's back onto terra firma. The
others joined her and they all looked with sympathy
at the dragon who was gloomily poking at the remains of the severed wing with one claw.

"Not easy to . . . gulp . . . fly with one wing," it
whimpered with self-pity and a black, oily tear
formed at the corner of one eye and rolled down to
splash onto the ground.

"Take it easy, old hoss," Mark I said with sadistic sympathy, extruding a large-bore cannon. "The

end of a wild dragon is always a tragedy. Close your eyes, you won't feel a thing. Saving us was a far, far better thing you did than you have ever done. The rest you go to now is a far, far better rest than . . ."

"Just put that shooter away, you unctuous metal bastard!" the dragon shouted, rearing back. "You're too quick on the draw." It began to eat the broken wing, glaring down at Mark I as it did. "I can grow a new one in a couple of weeks. Meanwhile I'm grounded."

"And so are we," Meta said, looking around at the verdant foliage. "At least this stuff looks a lot more homey than all that sand, coal, metal and oil . . ."

"Eeek!" the Fighting Devil eeked as it shivered and withdrew a test prod from a broken tree branch. "This is terrible. All this soft, gundgy stuff contains *water!* This is a poison plateau! We will rust, corrode, die in agony—"

"Oh shut up," the dragon suggested disgustedly, biting off a chunk of wood and swallowing it. "This stuff burns great. Just keep your extremities well oiled and watch where you sit down."

Bill's stomach growled and he nodded in agreement with it. "If we are going to be here a couple of weeks we are going to have to find food and water."

"All this repellent soft stuff contains water," Mark I said kicking the grass and shuddering. "If you eat that—"

"When I want dietary advice from a metal moron I'll ask for it," Meta said, turning on her heel. "Come on, Bill, we'll go find something. Fruits, vegetables—"

"You'll find the nasties who shot us down," the Fighting Devil said spitefully. "We metal morons will just stay here, vegetating, while you swan about through all that filthy muck. And *don't* hurry back."

Meta stuck her tongue out at it, took Bill by the arm and started down what looked like a path.

"That Fighting Devil is right," he said gloomily. "Who knows what hideous horrors lurk behind the jungle wall."

"You got your blaster—so blast them," Meta said with great practicality.

"The Chingers took it away. What about yours?"

"The same. Wait here, I got an idea."

She went back down the path while Bill listened to the noises of the jungle and chewed his fingernails. He was on his last pinky nail when she returned and handed him a strange looking weapon.

"I was right. That Fighting Devil is so loaded with artillery that it could break off a couple and not miss them. That's a lightning–bolt hurler you got there. Just aim and press the red button on top."

"Nice," he said, blowing the top off of an innocent tree. "What do you have?"

"Gravity beam. It trebles the mass of anything you shoot. Immobilizes it until the charge wears off."

"That's heavy stuff. We are going to be OK."

"Well if the truth be known, you are not," the red man said stepping out of the undergrowth, pointing a long and ugly weapon at them. "I would be truly obliged if you'all would hand over the hardware thus guaranteeing your safety. You have my word, as a southern gentleman, that you won't get hurt."

Meta would not give up without a struggle. She jumped aside and aimed her weapon—and found the point of a sword pinking her lightly in the throat.

"One twitch of your delicate pink trigger-finger, Ma'am, and you have bought the farm. Drop it."

The gun in his other hand was still pointing steadily at Bill. They had no choice. As soon as he had kicked their weapons aside the red man slipped his sword back into its sling, lowered his weapon and bowed politely.

"Welcome to Barthroom," he said in a soft southern accent. "Strangers are not welcome here, so may ah compliment you on your very good luck that you encountered me upon yore arrival. Mah name is Major Jonkarta late of the Confederate Forces, and ah claim Virginia as my home. And though I may resemble a native of this world—I am not. I came from a distant planet. I was pursued by aborigines; I sought refuge in a cave where ah fell asleep. There was witchcraft there, ah do believe, my spirit left my body, came here..."

"Whatever you have been smoking has got a real kick to it," Meta said. "The galaxy is full of psychos with identity problems, mothers impregnated by gods, changelings, noble infants stolen at birth..."

"What are you—a shrink or something?" Jonkarta pouted—then beamed with pleasure. "But mah dear, if you really are a specialist in problems of adjustment, Doctor, I have been having these awfully strange dreams..."

"My name is Engine Mate First Class Meta Tarsil. Meta to my friends—and you can be one too if you knock off the mystic crap."

"Why you just consider it done, Meta honey! Ah just love your strength..."

"Do I get to talk too? I'm Second Lieutenant Bill of the Space Troopers."

"How very nice for you, military rank and everything. Well, welcome you all."

Introductions out of the way they had a chance to examine each other. Jonkarta examined Meta—who was far better to look at than Bill who was getting decidedly scruffy. Meta thought so too and found herself growing more and more interested in the newcomer. He was tall and broad shouldered, with plenty of red skin showing because of the clothes he was not wearing. No clothes at all, but wore instead a harness, sort of a modified horse's harness with buckles, jewels, daggers and things hanging from it. The only clothes, per se, that he wore was a kinky riveted mini athletic supporter. Well filled she noted, eyes glowing. Leather boots, rippling muscles, smart swagger, he was really something to write home to mother about. Though she wouldn't do that because mother might want one too.

"So—when all the eyeballing is done, you get to tell me what you are doing here," Jonkarta said.

"We were shot down," Bill said. "Did you have anything to do with that?"

"You ain't just whistling Dixie, pardner. Ah did it with mah own little radium rifle. This here plateau is more than a little short of raw materials so anytime one of those machines flap over we just blast it. Use the metal to make swords, guns, knives, bombs, you know the sort of thing."

"We sure do," Meta said. "But don't you have any metal left over for cheese-graters, colanders, tubas or baby rattles?"

"Ah admire your quickness of mind, Meta honey. You sure can't make war with colanders."

"You wouldn't mind telling us, Rusty, who—what, or which—you are at war with?"

"Why it's ma pleasure. There are two intelligent species that inhabit this plateau. One more intelligent than the other, it goes without saying. There are the red men of Barthroom, and the revolting, hideous and very smelly green men of Barthroom. These repugnant critters can be easily identified, even in the dark, not only by their smell but because they have four arms. And tusks just like you, Bill. Which makes me slightly suspicious."

"Count the arms!" Bill said angrily. "Anyway, four arms and green, that's just like the Chingers. Maybe they are related."

"Might ah inquire—who are these Chingers?"

"The enemy we are at war with."

"War? My, my. Now don't you tell me that you fight them with baby rattles and colanders?" He winked at Meta when he said this. She sniffed.

"So we got a war too. Doesn't mean we have to like it."

"Well ah shore like mine. Ah come from a long line of fighting men . . ."

"Listen," Bill said, raising his voice to be heard over the loud borborygmus of his empty stomach. "It has been a very long time since we ate last. Could we have this chat over dinner—if you know where we can find dinner."

"No problem. Food aplenty—as soon as you enlist."

"There's always a catch."

"Not in this one. Here, look at this nice cut of meat." He unclipped a leather bag from his harness and from it took a smoked thoat ham. "Might ah suggest a short service commission. Just one foray and you get an honorable discharge. And it's a mission of mercy as well."

"I just joined," Meta said as she grabbed for the meat. "Gimme."

"Me too!"

Jonkarta stepped back as they reached for the ham, half drawing his sword. "Just a moment longer, ah beg of you. The oath first. Place your right hand over your heart—you do have hearts? Good. And repeat after me. Ah swear by Great Embollizm, ruler of the sun and the stars, overseer of Barthroom, protector of the red men, enemy of the green men, sure death on the white apes, giver of gifts, protector of all, that ah will be loyal to Jonkarta of Barthroom, and all who serve under him, will obey all orders and shower at least once a week."

They repeated, choking on the saliva that filled their mouths as they smelled the succulent thoat flesh, then eagerly grabbed the chunks he hacked off with his sword.

"Mighty fine vittles, is it not? Smoked it myself. And while you munch I'll tell you what we must do. It seems that Princess Dejah Vue, whom ah am passionately in love with, was returning from the air plant, where all the air on this planet is made, when her party was attacked by a marauding war party of cruel green men led by the cruelest of all. Tars Tookus. Her companions were all butchered horribly, her riding thoat was killed—you just ate part of it, ah didn't want it to go to waste—and she was abducted by Tars Tookus and his repellent horde."

"Were you there?" Bill asks miffedly.

"No. To mah everlastin' regret ah arrived on the scene too late—or none of those fiends would have survived. I read all that transpired in their tracks in the trackless moss for ah am a mighty hunter and tracker. No other could find a trail in the moss. I alone, trained by Apache warriors..."

"Could we save the ego-trip until later?" Meta implored.

"You are correct, Ma'am, ah do apologize. Where was I?"

"Tracking the green girl-grabbers across the trackless wastes."

"Yes, of course. I could not attack their encampment singlehandly, so I was returning to the city of Methane for reinforcements when ah heard your voices. By enlisting your aid I will save many days march and we can take them by surprise."

Meta swallowed the last morsel and wiped her hands on the tall grass. "Got anything to wash that down with?"

"Of a certainty, Ma'am." He handed her his leathern drinking bottle and she glugged deeply. "That is kvetch, made from fermented thoat's milk."

"Tastes like it too," she yekked, spitting out lumps of it. "How many of these greenies do we have to fight?"

"One, two, more. Ah'm not so good at mah numbers. Just killing."

"One or two, OK," Bill said, gagging on the kvetch. "We can handle that. If it is going to be a big number, like *more,* we are going to need help. You better enlist our friend back there, Mark I Fighting Devil."

"That is rightly an ugly and dangerous critter,

that is why ah did not approach. Is it your metal slave?"

"Hardly. But it will obey orders. Wait here and I'll bring it back."

The dragon, which had polished off all the broken branches and was contentedly puffing green smoke, was now working on the hanging vines; a length of one hung like spaghetti from its mouth. It waved a languid paw at Bill and pulled down another vine.

Fighting Devil was not enjoying its stay quite as well. It sat on a dry rock with its legs tucked up under it.

"Got some work for you," Bill said, but it never moved.

"Is it dead?" Bill asked the dragon.

"Not quite. Got its power shut down to save its batteries."

"That's great. How do I get to talk to it then?"

"Seems pretty obvious. Use the phone."

Bill walked around the rock and saw that there was a metal box on its back with strange and cabalistic characters stamped on it.

"Is this it? Looks like AT&T."

"You got it in one."

Bill broke his last remaining nail prying the box open. He took out the handset and spoke into it.

"Hello—anyone home?" It crackled and rustled in his ear.

"This is a recorded message. The Fighting Devil is powered down right now. If you would like to leave a message it will get back to you as soon as possible . . ."

"Show some life, will you. We got work to do." But the response was only silence. Bill cursed and put the phone back on the hook, slammed the box shut. Then he saw that the open lid had concealed a red button labeled FOR EMERGENCY USE ONLY.

"That's more like it," he said and pressed hard.

The results were quite dramatic. The Fighting Devil's legs punched down hard and shot the creature high into the air. As it fell sheets of raw energy crackled lambently, shells burst in the surrounding forest, while a siren hooted insanely.

Bill dived behind the dragon as bullets clanged off its metal hide.

"I tried to warn you," the dragon said. "But you were so impetuous."

"What's the emergency?" Fighting Devil shouted, spinning its optics in all directions.

"There's no emergency," Bill said, hesitantly leaving cover. "I wanted to talk to you . . ."

"That's what the phone is for. It is a violation to press the emergency button if there is no . . ."

"Will you please shut up and listen! We've got a little job to do."

"Since when? All I have to do is sit on my can for a couple of weeks while the dragon regenerates its wing. How is it going?"

Fighting Devil extended a pickup towards the dragon who pointed with a claw at a metal bulge on its side. "Going great."

Bill was getting angry. "Listen here, Fighting Devil, it's time to live up to your name. We got more to do than sit around and watch the dragon's wing grow. There's a war going on out there."

"You're welcome to it. Powering down now. All systems gone. Ten . . . nine . . ."

"Hold it! You were ordered to take orders from me!"

"No way, squishy one. I was ordered by the great Zots to rescue the other squishy and bring you both back alive. That's the limit of my responsibility. Night-night..."

"No! Hold it right there. You've got to bring us back, right? And we have to wait here for two weeks. But if Meta and I don't eat we'll die. Now we have made a deal for food in exchange for a little bit of fighting. But we need your help, get that? So you have to come with us."

"Impeccable chain of logic I would say," the dragon said. "I'll be here when you get back."

You could hear the wheels spinning as Mark I tried to think of a way out of this one. There was no escape. Lights came on and motors hummed as it switched back to full power.

"Well," it said, with philosophic resignation. "It's better for a Fighting Devil to fight than to estivate—so let's get on with the job. Where's the war?"

CHAPTER 13

JONKARTA WAS VERY SUSPICIOUS OF BILL'S companion. He stood behind Meta, sword in one hand, his weapon in the other.

"Don't come any closer, hear!" he ordered. "This here rifle fires radium bullets that will go right through your tin friend."

Meta shied away from him. "Are you crazy or something? *Radium?* You must glow in the dark— and have the life expectancy of a gerbil!"

"Ah admit that the new radium bullets do glow in the dark—and explode in the dark as well. So beware! The old ones, fired at night, did not explode until the sun's rays struck them next day. But no more. Can you trust that creature?"

"It obeys orders—and that's enough. Now put that gun down. And stay as far away from us as possible."

"If this metal critter is to join the cause it must take an oath of allegiance..."

"Never!" Fighting Devil boomed out in a brazen voice. "Loyalty cannot be subdivided and I have sworn an oath in oil to golden Zots, my liege lord. But I will follow and I will obey instructions in order to keep my ward, this squishy one here, alive —so you are going to have to settle for that, bud."

"Ah'm not sure . . ."

"Well I am," Bill said, tired of the entire stupid argument. "And this thing is not human in any case, it's just a machine . . ."

"I am not 'just a machine'!" Fighting Devil grated.

"Hold it there!" Meta shouted, but no one was listening. "There's one way to settle this," she muttered, raised her weapon and shot all three of them.

The shouting ended at once. Bill and Jonkarta instantly fell to the ground, dragged down by the three gravities projected by the gun. Even Fighting Devil ground its gears helplessly. Meta sat on a fallen log and hummed to herself as she wove a circlet of wild flowers. As the charge wore off they began to stir and moan. She patted the flowers into place on her head, stood and stretched.

"Now that the argument is over—can we maybe get this war over with as well?"

"We march," Jonkarta ordered, pouting slightly at being put down by a mere woman. "You will find their encampment just one day's journey from here, at the edge of the long-dead city of Mercaptan. We will take up our positions in darkness. The battle will be joined at dawn."

"You're the boss," Meta said. "Lead on. And could I have another slug of that fermented thoat's milk, just for the road."

Jonkarta knew every path and trail in the jungle and on the mossy plain and went silently on little cat's feet. (He had killed the little cat and skinned it and used its feet to make soles for his moccasins. An old Barthroomian custom that brings good luck. But not to the cat.) Unknown dangers lurked here, but as soon as they made themselves known they were blasted by Fighting Devil who was now enjoying itself. Very quickly fragments of giant python, wolverine-possum, as well as bits of the hideous latke-eater, littered the ground. Jonkarta was more relaxed now, seeing that the newcomers really were fighting on his side.

"Ah must say, you really are a fighting devil," he said.

"Eponymous, that's me," it agreed and shots rang out as it blew away a charging nenitesk.

Because their explosive passage expedited their journey through the forest they reached the edge of the great mossy wastes just as the sun was setting behind the distant edge of the plateau.

"They are there," Jonkarta said, pointing grimly, which is not easy to do. "You can make out the dark forms of their tents, the even darker forms of the grazing thoats . . ."

"Speaking of thoats," Meta interjected, "I'll have a bit more of that ham."

"You think more of your stomach than you do of mah darling Dejah Vue!"

"Right now, yes, Red. Eat first, fight later."

Since Fighting Devil needed no sleep it took the first watch that night. Then the second and the third, and woke them just before dawn.

"What's your plan, Jonkarta?" Bill asked after they had broken their fast with the last of the ham and snuck out behind the trees to make peepee.

"There is but one plan—fight and win!"

"Brilliant." Fighting Devil was not impressed. "But if you want some advice on fighting from an experienced Fighting Devil you ought to organize things a little bit better than that. How many of them are there?"

"Countless hordes!"

"You wouldn't like to be a *little* more precise?"

"Don't bother," Bill said. "I've danced this one before. This lad counts one, two, more."

"Ah'm a better shot than you are paleface," Jonkarta sulked. "Ah don't need to count—just fight!"

"You'll fight, you'll fight," Fighting Devil bemoaned, fed up with all soft, wet aliens. "Let's make this simple. What do you say I walk in there and blow everyone away?"

"You will kill mah darling princess!"

"OK, we modify the plan. You sneak in now under cover of darkness and find where she is. Then when I arrive at dawn you point to her tent and I blow everything else away."

"But how do I find her in the darkness?"

"Use your nose," Meta said, fed up with the bickering. "If she doesn't stink you can smell her out among the smellies."

"Stink! Were you not female you would be dead. My darling has the aroma of sweet roses, delicate dafs, all the fair flowers..."

"Terrific. Sniff out this bouquet of beauty and let trigger-happy know which tent she is in. Can we now get this war on the road?"

"Ah will now seek out my darling. Silence is the word so ah dare not take Ol' Betsy here, mah trusty radium rifle. Ah leave it in yore care, Ma'am..."

"No way! Hang it from a tree and it will be here when you get back."

Jonkarta had no choice. He secured the weapon high in a ginja tree, then silent as a wraith slipped out into the desert.

Fighting Devil hummed to itself as the sky

lightened in the west—the planet of Usa rotated backward—as it reloaded all its weapons and charged up the ray projectors. Bill stretched out to get a quick thirty winks, it had been a long night, but Meta had better ideas. She crept under the shrouding shrub that concealed him, settled beside him on the soft moss and the night was filled with the music of zippers being unzipped. And being re-zipped when they saw an infrared detector protruding from the shrub.

Meta grabbed for it but it slipped away. "If vegetative reproduction is your bag," she shouted, "how come this big interest in heterosexuality?"

"Maybe I feel frustrated. Sun's up. The lark's on the wing, the thoat on the thand. Here I go!"

The camp was already astir, and it astirred even more at the sight of Fighting Devil trundling towards them. A horde of ravenous, verminous, carious green martians poured out of the tents roaring evil oaths and firing at their metal attacker. Fighting Devil raised its guns and aimed them, but held its fire.

"Soft red squishy one—where are you?"

"Here," Jonkarta said, raising his head out of a ditch—and ducking again when radium bullets began to whistle by. "Kill as you will—but spare the tent with the mark of the beast on it."

"I'm afraid that I'm not familiar with the term."

Jonkarta quickly traced 666 in the sand. "It looks like that."

"Gotcha." Fighting Devil aimed its electronic telescope, ignoring the bullets clanging on its hide, and swept the line of tents. "I've found it—and here I go!"

It was very dramatic. The grotesque green men

never stood a chance before the maelstrom of fire and bullets. Stormed at by shot and shell, they all exploded well. Gobbets of green flesh flew in all directions and thudded into the sand among the debris of broken tents, fur rugs, silken drapes, gold bangles, contraceptives, pistols and swords, portapotties—all the things that made life in the harsh desert possible. Meta and Bill, hand in hand, came to watch the noisy demonstration of invincible firepower. Within instants the proud camp was a smoking ruin—from which a single tent projected. It was unharmed, although it was well spattered with green blood.

"Mah darlin' Dejah Vue—is she safe?"

"You bet," Fighting Devil bragged. "I never miss." It extruded a compressed air hose and blew the smoke from a smoking gun muzzle.

"Ahm here, darlin', longing for your embrace!" Jonkarta cried leaping forward and throwing wide the tent flap.

Then he screamed in agony as a giant green monster leaped out and trod him to the ground.

"You have destroyed my entire tribe!" he bellowed and beat his great chest. "I thirst for vengeance and your blood!"

"Tars Tookus . . . you were in the tent, alone—with her! What have you done with my loved one?"

"Guess!" the jolly green giant leered through his tusks as it leaped aside. "Draw—and defend yourself!"

Jonkarta's sword leaped to his hand—which is easier than drawing it—and he roared and attacked. But Tars Tookus had drawn his sword. Swords. All four of them, which is okay if you have four arms. Undaunted, Jonkarta pressed home his attack, so furiously that his sword was a whirring circle of steel that forced the green warrior back despite his four to one advantage. When they were clear of the tent Jonkarta called out for aid.

"Bill—to the tent! See if any harm has befell my loved one!"

Bill circled the battling warriors and poked his head into the tent and stood, paralyzed.

"How is . . . she?" Jonkarta gasped out between crashing blows.

"She—she looks really great to me!"

And she did. Lolling back on the silken cushions, Dejah Vue was the acme of female beauty. Her delicate red skin—and there was a lot of it showing —glowed with health and desirability. Mere wisps of transparent and diaphanous cloth revealed rather than concealed her rounded charms. Breasts like melons fought for freedom.

"Are you . . . are you all right?" Bill husked.

"Come here and find out," she husked in turn.

As the tentflap fell behind him the fierce battle was drawing to a close. Even with four swords, Tars Tookus was no match for Jonkarta's superior swordsmanship. His upper right arm tired and his opponent sensed it and lunged forward, parrying the sword aside and, with one mighty blow, cut the green man's head off. Jonkarta roared with victory as the gigantic figure collapsed into an immobile heap, green blood spurting from the severed neck.

"Thus die all those who dare come between me and my loved one!" he crowed victoriously, spun about and threw wide the tentflap. And roared in anger when he saw what was happening inside.

"Thus die all those who dare come between me

and my loved one!" he cried out yet again and rushed in.

"I was just examining her to see if she was wounded!" Bill cried out, dodging behind the red princess before he could get pierced through and through.

"Out coward! Out of the tent and fight like a man!"

Meta and Fighting Devil looked on with great interest as Bill came shooting out of the tent with the frothing Jonkarta a step behind him. Meta put her foot out when the red man passed and the raging warrior fell on his mush.

"Shame on you, attacking an unarmed man. If you are going to duel, do it by the rules. Bill's choice of weapons."

"You are right of course," Jonkarta said climbing to his feet and brushing off a few gobbets of green flesh. He folded his arms and glowered at Bill. "Choose. Radium rifles at twenty paces. Daggers, pistols, swords, maces—the choice is yours. But decide at once for I cannot contain my rage for long."

Dejah Vue joined the other spectators, drawing a diaphanous wisp of cloth over her charms that inflamed men's minds. Meta glared down her nose at her, sniffed and turned away. *Fat,* she thought. *She'll need a girdle before she hits thirty.*

All eyes were on Bill now—and he did not like it. He had seen what this muscle-bound ape had done against a giant with four arms. "I know," he said. "Finger-wrestling!"

"Weapons, your choice of!" Jonkarta roared in anger. He kicked one of the fallen swords towards his opponent. "And you have just run out of time.

Pick that up and defend yourself—or say a quick last prayer before I run you through."

"Help me, faithful Fighting Devil," Bill begged. "Stop this madman from murdering me."

"Not my fight, buster. I was sent out to bring Meta back alive—and that I will do. You get into trouble messing with the local girls—that's your problem."

"Meta . . .?"

"You want this pudgy thing—you fight for her. I'll watch."

"Time is up," Jonkarta said with grim pleasure as he aimed his sword at Bill's belly button. "Is that where your heart is?"

"No, here," Bill said tapping his chest, then jerked his hand away. "I mean, no, you can't do this . . ."

Iron biceps tensed. The sword started forward.

And Dejah Vue screamed a piercing scream and they turned as one to see her in the loathsome grip of Tars Tookus.

"But-but—" Jonkarta butted, "I just cut off your head."

"Ha-ha! And so you did," the green warrior leered and gestured towards the stump of his neck with one of his free hands. "But what you *didn't* know is that I have two heads, the other was tied down my back so you couldn't see it. When your attention was diverted I tied a tourniquet around this stump, freed my second head—and have captured this wench." He whistled shrilly and a great thoat galloped up on six legs.

"You dare not shoot for fear of hitting my captive," he cried victoriously as he bounded into the saddle, the screaming princess pressed tight to his noisome body. "And now I go! I do not kill you, but leave you instead to visualize what her fate will be!"

His maniacal laughter was drowned out by the muted thud of thoat's hooves on the moss as they vanished over the horizon.

CHAPTER 14

"AFTER MAH DARLIN'!" JONKARTA BELLOWED. "We must save her."

"We just did," Meta told him. "If you had cut off both of Tars Tookus's heads we wouldn't be having this problem."

"How was ah to know he had two heads? Ahm no prevert—ah never looked at his back! We must follow them—after ah butchers this philanderer!"

His sword whistled a deadly tune as it flashed in the warm Barthroomian sunshine. Bill raised his gun and pulled the trigger. A lightning bolt flashed from the muzzle and blew the sword from the red man's hand.

"That ain't fair!" Jonkarta howled, then poured some kvetch over his burnt palm. "Yore no gentleman."

"Damn right—I'm an enlisted man, although temporarily an officer."

"Mah sword seeks to drink yore blood . . ."

Once more Meta had to resort to her gravity pistol to stop the argument. While both men lay gasping on the moss she looked into the tent. It was heaped with moldy furs and stained silks and stank of green man. There was a sealed bottle that she first sniffed at, then drank from and smacked her lips.

She carried it out to see that Bill was sitting up wearily.

"Try some of this—it's better than the kvetch."

He glugged happily as Jonkarta came around. He sniffed the air and cried aloud.

"That smell? What are you all drinking?" Meta held out the bottle and he cried aloud, and not for the first time. "The incredibly rare perfume of the shtunkox vine that blossoms but once a century, so precious that . . ."

"You want a slug or do you want to lecture?" Meta asked with touching sympathy. "It's got alcohol in it. That's it, incredibly rare, knock it back. And no more talk of polishing off Bill. I've had enough of this macho crap. You can have your duel—then go on alone. Or forget the whole thing and you got a small army, namely us and Fighting Devil. What's it going to be?"

"Mah darling's life comes ahead of mah honor . . ."

"That's a speedy bit of rationalizing. So what do we do next?" she asked, taking command, fed up with men for the moment.

"We will use their thoats to follow them. The creatures lack saddle or bridle and are directed by telepathy."

"An unlikely story."

"If they act unruly you must beat their skull with the butt of your pistol."

"Sounds dangerous—but I'll try everything once. Fighting Devil, you circle around the thoats and move them in our direction."

The sight of one red Barthroomian, two pinkish humans and a metallic Fighting Devil rounding up a herd of twenty-foot long, six-legged, oversexed thoats is one best left undescribed. Suffice to say that too much later four brain-damaged thoats, they had been beat about the head too much, staggered across the trackless plain bearing their fatigued and moss-covered riders.

"Let us not do that again...soon..." Meta gasped. Then pointed and shrieked. "We're being attacked!"

A hideous, pallid, ten-legged creature was hurtling towards them, salivating as it charged. It had three rows of long, sharp tusks, which meant it had to keep its mouth open like it had adenoids. Because there was no way it could close it with all that bad-fitting dentition in the way.

It bounded forward, leapt high into the air and crashed into Jonkarta.

Who scratched its head while it panted and drooled down his harness front.

"This is mah faithful hound, Rayona. It must have run day and night for two weeks to get here. These creatures are tireless."

Rayona promptly dropped unconscious and began to snore, draped across the thoat's back.

"We march," Jonkarta gasped as he pushed the dead weight off his legs which were being crushed. "That way, towards the dead city of Mercaptan on the shores of the Dead Sea. Pray to your alien gods that we are not too late."

They galloped off, and as they ran Fighting Devil directed his thoat to Meta's side. It obeyed its rider's every wish—it had no choice with a cannon in each ear. Fighting Devil was quite itself and was posting very nicely.

"An unusual experience. I will have quite a tale to tell back in the Fighting Devil's mess with my mates. What was that red squishy talking about, alien gods or some such? He has such a thick rebel accent that it is hard to follow him at times."

"Not . . . now, Fighting Devil. If you think I am going to explain comparative religion to a metal life form while thundering across a dead ocean bottom on a six-legged thoat's back—you are out of your gourd."

They galloped most of the day, since Jonkarta would not heed their cries for a break. He only called a halt when the crumbled towers of Mercaptan appeared ahead. They all, with the exception of Fighting Devil of course, rolled off onto the soft moss gasping with relief. The thoats began to graze and the faithful hound, Rayona, woke up and broke wind.

They forgot their fatigue and ran for safety, all except Fighting Devil who had no sense of smell.

"Here is my plan," Jonkarta said after the air had cleared and he had kicked the faithful hound's ass around the moss for awhile. "We must take them by surprise since we are outnumbered. I know a secret way in . . ."

"Why surprise?" Meta asked, surprised. "Why don't we just send Fighting Devil in like last time and blow them all away?"

"Because now they are warned. At the first gunshot they will kill my darlin'. That must not be! We will slip through the upper stories of the deserted buildings, which move they will never suspect."

"Why not?" Bill asked, getting more confused all the time.

"Because these upper stories are inhabited by the hideous white apes, giant fearsome creatures that lust to kill."

"Won't they lust to kill us?" Meta asked.

"I suppose so," Jonkarta pouted. "I never thought of that. I know! If they attack your metal warrior will kill them."

"Smart. Explosions and bang-bang upstairs. The gruesome greenies will never notice that."

"I can do it," Fighting Devil said. "I have silent death-rays, coagulator rays that turn a body hard like a hard-boiled egg, poison gas, that sort of thing. Want a demonstration?"

"Demonstrate on the white apes," Bill said. "Shall we do it before it gets too late?"

Jonkarta led the way. Into a ruined building and up the great staircase, ever upward until they reached the full garbage pails of the top floor. They made their way through one room, then another—and found their nemesis in the third room they entered.

"There!" Jonkarta shouted fearfully. "The hideous great white ape. Kill!"

"White ape indeed!" the creature roared back. "And that from you, you red commie bastard. I'll give you five of the best where it will do the most good!"

"Wait," Bill said, laying a restraining hand on Fighting Devil's gunbarrel as it surged malevolently forward. "Don't fire yet. That creature appears to be able to talk."

"Creature indeed! And who are you to come barging into a man's parlor with a murderous looking machine and this red idiot. And a fair young colleen, I must admit, to make the party complete."

"Kill!" Jonkarta ordered and the murderous form of the ten-legged hound hurtled forward.

"Down," the white ape ordered. "Heel. Nice doggy. Here's a bone for you." The skull of a thoat dropped to the floor and was instantly seized by Rayona and a great crunching followed.

"My name is Meta," she said, stepping forward. "I hope you don't mind our barging in like this."

"Not at all, not at all! An Lar is the name, but my friends call me An. Or Lar. Or An Lar. The wife and kiddies are out shopping. We're having roast leg of green Barthroomian tonight and you can join us if you like."

"Why thank you. I'll ask my friends." She spun about and glared at Fighting Devil who sulkily retracted its weapons. "As you can plainly see these so-called white apes are human—or close to it."

"Human we are, without a doubt, may Samedi strike me down if that's not true."

"Samedi?" Bill said, dim memories surging up from his rusty synapses. "Somehow, familiar. A friend of mine used to talk about Samedi. A Trooper named Tembo."

"Named after St. Tembo, bedad, one of the holy saints of The First Reformed Voodoo Church. And where is your friend now?"

"Here. Or at least part of him is. He was killed in action. I lost an arm in the same battle. This is his arm, all that was left of him. It gives me something to remember him by."

"Well sure and put it there!" Bill's left arm shot up of its own volition. "Faith and I was wondering why you had one black arm and one white arm, both of them right arms at that, but I didn't think it polite to ask. Come in, all of you, it's a rare thing to see a friendly face these days. Sure and it was a black day when the ship crashed on this accursed planet."

"Ship? Crashed?" Bill echoed.

"Aye. A great spacer packed with refugees from

the planet Earth, if you can believe the old stories. It is said that it was on this ship that the great conversion took place. Although those who boarded were of many religions, when they disembarked of religions there was but one. Due to the zealous missionary work of St. Tembo, hallowed be his name."

"That's what Tembo always said," Bill said. "That Earth was destroyed by an atomic war, at least the northern hemisphere was."

"Sure and tis nice to have a little verification of the old stories. Myths the youngsters call them—and they sneer. But it's no myth that we are stranded on this barren planet. We raise a few potatoes in the roof gardens, eat a green Barthroomian or two when we get hungry. Begorrah and it's a rough life—made even rougher by the likes of him calling us apes!"

"I'm sorry. As a Southern gentleman ah do apologize. Just repeating what I heard."

"Shows just how wicked rumor can be. But tell me, what brings you to our fair city?"

"My fiancée, the lovely Princess Dejah Vue, has been captured by the foul creatures that lurk below. We must free her!"

"Well you have come to right place, boyo, if it's a little freeing and green Barthroomian bashing you want. And besides, the meat locker is empty. You just wait here, give another bone to that starving hound, and I'll be back in three shakes of a thoat's tail."

"He's nice," Meta said after their host had swung out of the window.

True to his word he was back almost as quickly as he had left, but his great white brow was puckered with worry.

"Begorrah and it's not going to be that easy. I think they know that you are coming?"

"What makes you say that?"

"Signs saying *To the kidnaped Princess* all over the city. 'Tis me firm opinion that they'll be waiting for you."

"That's the way I want it," Jonkarta said grimly, resolutely clutching his sword. "If they think they can capture me then they won't harm her. So we attack."

Meta was shocked. "You mean walk right into the trap?"

"We have no other choice."

"He's right, we have no choice," Bill and An Lar intoned together.

"That's what you male macho morons say." Meta's lips curled with well-justified disgust. "But speaking from the female point of view I say reconnoiter first. There is always plenty of time to die later."

"No," Fighting Devil boomed. "Fight first, think later. I may not be male, vegetative propagation is asexual, but by Zots I like this macho talk. Let's go!"

"All gonads no brains," Meta said disgustedly as they marched out. She followed at a watchful distance and stayed in the building above when they tramped out into the central square.

"It is empty! They have fled because they fear us!" Jonkarta cried out and the others cheered.

Then the ground opened up and they fell into the pit below while countless green Barthroomians poured out of the surrounding buildings, shouting victory cries and laughing and making obscene gestures which, with four arms working at once, are really pretty obscene.

"Told you so," Meta sniffed. "But no one listens to me."

Then her heart fell and she clasped her hands in despair.

"Is it all over? Is this how life ends? Not with a bang but with a green Barthroomian massacre and barbecue."

She sighed tremulously and the only sound in the room was the crunch of hideous mighty fangs gnawing on a thoat bone. Followed by a hideous belch of satisfaction.

CHAPTER 15

MEANWHILE, BACK IN THE CITY OF METAL, Zots was beginning to get worried.

"They should have been back by now. I fear for your associates." He took a swig of high-octane petrol to quiet his nerves and watched the admiral busily at work.

"Relax, Goldy," Praktis muttered as he unscrewed a bolt from the hapless machine that he had nailed to the floor. It clicked its loudspeaker with agony. Praktis pointed to Wurber who handed him a wrench. Captain Bly was there as well, watching him, watching unseeingly, his head bobbing. Although they had cleaned out most of his supplies they had not found the stash of dope in the hollow heel of his boot. So he had popped an upper, a downer, and a sider, and was really spaced out of it.

"I would like to relax, thank you," Zots suffered. "But I am so ashamed of my lack of hospitality. First there was one, but now two of your associates are missing."

"Two, two hundred. I've lost more people than that doing illegal research on the common cold. Aha!"

The machine screeched as its leg came off. Praktis leaned forward and focused his microscopic eye on the socket. Zots looked pained. "I wish you could stop when I am talking to you. At your request I have supplied you with machines for dissection—I mean examination. But I would appreciate it if you would wait until I leave."

"Sorry." Praktis straightened up and tucked his black monocle back into place. "I do tend to get carried away with my work. Where's Cy?"

"Here," he said, carrying in a tray of steaming steaks. "Food. I'm hungry. You?"

"Well, perhaps a little." Praktis took a bite and pushed it away. "I like meat on the menu as well as the next man—but this is beginning to get boring. I should have worked on quick-grow artichokes, or maybe mangel-wurzels . . ."

He was interrupted by sharp screeching sounds as the machine he had been examining pulled out the nails that had been holding it down. It hopped frantically away on one leg.

"Stop!" Praktis shouted.

"Let it go," Zots said. "There are plenty more where it came from. Now, if I might return to the topic under discussion. Your missing companions. Our detectors have picked up a faint transponder signal from somewhere in the badlands. It seems to be the correct frequency for a Mark I Fighting Devil. Therefore I have sent for an improved Mark II model. Which, if I am not mistaken, is here now."

The door was thrown open with a great crash and the Fighting Devil ran into the room, circled it twice and shot a hole in the wall, then subsided panting with pleasure. Zots nodded agreement.

"Much improved, through selected breeding. We took cuttings. Pushed a few genes around, you know the kind of thing. So now they are more aggressive, better armored, more firepower, bigger batteries, smaller brains."

"That's me!" the Fighting Devil shouted happily and blew away half of the ceiling. Praktis looked on disgustedly and did not notice Wurber stealing the rest of his steak.

"What are we supposed to do with it?" he asked.

"Mount a rescue mission of course. If you will follow me I will lead you to the ornithopter."

"Not me—I'm the admiral here." He looked around and sneered at the spaced out Captain Bly. "We seem to be running out of troops. You there, Corporal Cy BerPunk, you just volunteered for the rescue mission."

"Negative, no go. I can't take heights. Get Wurber. Afraid."

"Wurber's too stupid. And you are more afraid of me. Go!"

Cy fingered his blaster and wondered if might not be wiser to blow Praktis away rather than go on this suicide mission. But the admiral had plenty of experience with reluctant troops, volunteers and patients, so he made his mind up far more quickly. "Lookee, lookee," he smiled, aiming his gun between the unwilling volunteer's eyes. "Just follow Fighting Devil and return with your shipmates. Go."

Reluctantly, he went. Fighting Devil II led the way at a trot, extending an eye on a stalk to look at his new companion. "I'm so excited—this is my first mission."

"Shut up."

"Don't talk bad to Fighting Devil or Fighting Devil blow you up."

"Sorry. Nerves. I'm easy. Lead the way."

An ornithopter was waiting in the courtyard for them. Little service machines were oiling its wing sockets and brushing its teeth.

"We go now," Fighting Devil grated and dismissed the attendant machines.

"Maybe," the ornithopter said in a deep voice. "Your bunch of nuts flew my sister out of here and she never came back. Where are we supposed to go?"

"Go badlands."

"Forget it! No suicide missions for me."

A bolt of lightning shot out of Fighting Devil's crotch and burnt a foot of metal off the ornithopter's tail.

The ornithopter looked back its tail and smiled insincerely.

"You know, now that I think about it, I've always harbored a secret wish to see the badlands. Hop aboard."

"More willing volunteers," Cy gloomed. "I'm getting bad vibes from this mission."

"Be cheery, sloppy wet one," Fighting Devil said, pulling him up onto the flying creature's back. "We fly to battle! Kill, destroy!" It blew great pits in the ground behind them as they rattled into the air.

As flights go, this one went. The Fighting Devil hummed merry battle tunes to itself, occasionally firing off a gun in a high-spirited fashion, and tuning in on the distant transponder.

"Getting louder. Clearer. Point nose and flap towards black spot on horizon," it ordered.

The ornithopter rattled into a turn and felt more and more depressed as their destination grew clearer.

"I knew it," he moaned softly. "The Plateau of Doom."

"No plateau of doom on my map. And I got good maps."

"No map dares represent its inconceivably repellent form, transcribe its forbidden name."

"Then how you know?"

"It happened thusly. Visualize the happy scene. The Old Mob, sitting around the oil well in the evenings, talking lightly of this or that—when there is a sudden silence. All grows still as the oldesthopter speaks. Wings drooping, rivets popping, it regales the silent assembly with the Old Stories, passed on from generation to generation. And always, in the end, warns of the Plateau of Doom."

While it spoke the ornithopter had been drifting off course. Cy noticed it but hoped that the dim machine he was clutching would not. He had about as much enthusiasm as their mechanical steed for the plateau ahead.

"We turning!" Fighting Devil shouted. "Go that way, no go this way."

"It is sure death!"

"It surer death when me blow you out of sky!"

Guns blazed and wingtips flared into oblivion.

"You can't do that!" the ornithopter screeched. "If you shoot me down you will die too!"

More guns blazed, more bits of metal were blown off. Fighting Devil gave a mechanical shrug. "I know. But what can I do? After all, this is total war."

Weeping oily tears, the ornithopter winged over onto the original course. Cy wondered if he could possibly push the metal moron overboard, but saw that the thing was firmly bolted into place.

"Why you fly so high?" it asked.

"The higher we fly, the safer we are from the terrors below."

"I no see so good up here."

"Use your telescopic lenses—or did you forget?"

"Oh, yes! Me forget." The lens ground out and Cy began to believe that intelligence reduction, while normally a fine thing for the military mind, just wasn't working with this creature.

"Go thataway. Towards city of ruins. Signal strong. I send message. Ho, dear vegetatively propagated kinsman. Help on way!"

"Any answer?" Cy asked.

"Coming in now. PRISONER IN PIT STOP . . . Say, that pretty funny message. Why it in pit stop?"

"It's a telegram, dummy. It means it's in a pit. Then stop. Stop means period."

"Why not say period?"

"Is there any more?" Cy fought down his anger, fear, disgust and a lot of other things.

"Oh, yeah. SQUISHIES IN PIT WITH ME STOP SAVE US STOP ATTACK ATTACK ATTACK SOONEST ATTACK ATTACK."

"I think it wants you to attack."

"That's what I'm good at!" Guns banged wildly and Cy had to shout to be heard.

"Stop firing! You'll warn them—and you need the ammunition."

"Land there, carrying creature. Signal come from central square."

The ornithopter zoomed down behind the ruined buildings and slammed to the ground.

"You land wrong spot. Square there."

"Me land right spot. Save life of me and squishy. Go, mighty Fighting Devil! Attack!"

"Attack? Attack what?"

"The pit in the square with the captives!" Cy shouted with exasperation.

"Oh, *yeah*—that pit!"

It hurtled off and instants later the air was filled with explosives, screams, cries of pain, thunder of lightning bolts and such. Which died away pretty quickly.

"Did it win?" Cy whispered.

"Go look," the ornithopter whispered back.

"Let's toss for it. Loser goes to look."

"Don't bother," Meta whispered from the balcony above their heads. "I can see fine from up here. That Fighting Devil has fought its last fight. It did some damage, but it walked into the muzzles of a thousand radium rifles and is now radioactive junk. Come on up. Through the door and up the stairs."

The ornithopter trained one eye on the door. "Sorry. A little small for me. I'll just wait here and oil my wing sockets. Good luck."

Cy climbed the stairs and entered a large chamber filled with a milling crowd of pallid women. Meta sat behind a table at the far end of the room and was hammering with a gavel for order. When her voice could be heard she spoke to them again.

"We have been going over the same ground for some time now. A frontal attack just will not work. You just saw what happened to the Fighting Devil when it tried that."

"Wait til dark, then we bash them green meanies with our stone clubs."

"Not on your nelly!" another voice called out.

"The captives will be dead long before that. We must act now!"

Meta waved Cy forward. "Here!" she called out. "Reinforcements. He will help us."

"Glad to—if you will let me know what is going on."

"It is simple enough. Jonkarta, a native of Virginia now living on this planet, was crossing the desert with his betrothed, a red girl name of Princess Dejah Vue, when they were attacked by green Barthroomians who kidnapped the princess, but we arrived soon after and pursued the greenies and ambushed them, Fighting Devil blew them all away, except one that rekidnapped the princess and fled with her here, where we of course followed and attacked, but our forces, aided by this lady's husband, were defeated and captured, all except for me since I did not go along, and now they are all about to be tortured and executed."

"I'll not ask you to repeat that," Cy said, his head still ringing. "I have heard enough to know that the cause is hopeless. Why don't you and I grab the ornithopter and split?"

"Thanks very much, you sniveling coward," Meta sneered while the other women shook their fists and emitted howls of derision and hatred.

"Just trying to help," he shrugged.

"We can't just let them die!"

"The pallid young lady is right. Prepare to fire, chaps. Spare her life but shoot the rest of the hideous great white apes down," a strange voice said.

They all turned and gasped as a horde of red warriors, armed to the teeth, pushed in from the hallway, led by the speaker, also red, but also gray of head. They raised their guns to fire—but before they could all the women in the room dropped their stone clubs and from places of concealment whipped out radium rifles and aimed them at the intruders.

Cy yiped in the deadly silence that followed, trapped between the opposing forces. If he moved he might precipitate a massacre. Yet it seemed every gun was pointed at him. In desperation he spoke.

"Hold it! If one shot is fired we all die. And me first which is why I am negotiating this meeting. If you ruddy newcomers shoot you will be killing the captives who now await death in the square below..."

"And one of them is the Princess Dejah Vue," Meta added since the newcomers had the right color skin and might be co-religionists or co-countrymen of the prisoned plumpkin. Her guess hit the mark for the leader cried aloud, staggered back and hit his brow with the back of his hand. Meta smiled. "I have a feeling that you know the girl."

"Know her? She is my daughter! Order arms!" he shouted back over his shoulder. "I am Mors Orless Jeddak of Methane. She was overdue from a thoat tour and I was beginning to get worried. Then a telegram was intercepted from this city and filled my heart with fear. I assembled my army and came at once. Tell me, pallid one, what has happened?"

"It is simple enough. Jonkarta, a native of Virginia now living on this planet, was crossing the desert with his betrothed, a red girl name of Princess Dejah Vue, when they were attacked by green Barthroomians who kidnapped the princess, but we arrived soon after and pursued the greenies and ambushed them, Fighting Devil blew them all away, except one that rekidnapped the princess and fled with her here, where we of course followed and attacked, but our forces, aided by this lady's husband, were defeated and captured, all except for me since I did not go along, and now they are all about to be tortured and executed."

"We will save them! To arms, brave Methanians, to arms!"

"Hold it!" Meta shouted as they started to rush from the room. "Direct assault has already defeated a Fighting Devil, which is a very hard thing to do. We need a better plan than that."

"And sure and I've got just the darlin'est plan for yez," An Lar's wife said, stepping out before them, arms akimbo, the light of destiny in her eyes. "Here is what we shall do. We have been having a homophagic donnybrook with the green men for countless ages. Becuz they likes to eat us just as we like to eat them. So me, and the rest of the ladies, will go out unarmed and looking edible and throw ourselves on their mercy. Of course they have no mercy, but we'll make believe we don't know. They will not shoot us then but will instead attack with gusto, howling with hunger..."

"Whereupon," Mors Orless broke in with a wicked grin and a shake of his gray head, "we, who will be hiding behind every window around the square, will fire a withering barrage that will wipe out every one of the green sons of bitches!"

"For an old lad with the wrong skin color you're not too stupid! Shall we do it?"

Shouting shouts of untrammeled joy they streamed from the room, red men to their windows, white women to the square. The clouds of dust settled and Cy dragged wearily over and dropped into a chair across from Meta.

"This happen to you very often?"

"No. And once is enough."

Female shouts of submission echoed through the window, followed by hoarse bellows of happiness, and appetite. Which were soon replaced by the sound of gunfire and the screams of the mortally wounded. When this died away it was replaced by the sound of wild cheering. When the cheering, in turn, died away two voices could be heard calling in the ensuing silence.

"Jon!"

"Dejah!"

"JON!"

"DEJAH!"

"JON!!"

"DEJAH!!"

Louder and louder, accompanied by running footsteps, until it ended with the thud of colliding flesh. Followed by more cheers.

"Plan must have worked," Cy said.

Soon after this they heard weary footsteps dragging up the stairs and a much battered Fighting Devil staggered in half-supporting the equally battered body of Bill.

"We got an ornithopter waiting," Meta said, trying not to yawn. "What do you say we get the hell out of here."

CHAPTER 16

"YOU ARE DRIFTING OFF COURSE," FIGHTING
Devil said, kicking the ornithopter to get its attention. It stuck one eye out on its stalk and swiveled it
to see who was talking.

"How do you know?"

"Because I got a built-in direction finder."

"You're right, we are off course. But there is a
powerful force field that is drawing me towards
those mountains. I cannot fight it any longer. It is
bigger than me..."

"All right—save the histrionics." A large-bar-
reled cannon extruded from its chest. "Just fly towards
this mysterious force field and it will cease being a
mystery. I'll blast it. Everyone comfy back there?"

"No!" they chorused, clinging to the handholds,
jarred and vibrated to death.

"Poor soft squishy things," Fighting Devil tsk-
tsked with smarmy and obviously fake sympathy.
"How superior we metal-based creatures are... why
are we landing?"

"Because the power on the force field has been
turned up and I have no choice."

They were being drawn down towards a ledge
of rock, apparently empty of all life. Fighting Devil
blasted it anyway, but the force still pulled at them.

Even flapping at full flap the ornithopter could make no headway. In the end it was pulled down to the rocky surface, wings beating furiously and getting absolutely no place.

"Turn . . . off the . . . engine!" Bill gurgled and cried aloud and finally the wings slowed and stopped. While Fighting Devil was unbolting itself the human passengers slid to the ground with groans of pain and hobbled in circles, twisted and crunched.

"Never again!" Meta moaned. "Even if I have to spend the rest of my life on this mountain I'm not boarding that vibrating monster."

"Likewise," Cy sighed.

"Doubled in brass," Bill blurted.

"You are most welcome to stay."

"What said that?" Fighting Devil shouted, spinning about, all systems go, guns protruding from every orifice.

"None of us." Bill pointed. "It seemed to come from that tunnel there."

Fighting Devil instantly let fly with a barrage of shells that blew great chunks out of the cliff and sent fragments of stone flying in all directions.

"Knock it off!" Bill shouted, diving for cover.

When the firing had stopped the voice spoke again.

"Shame! I offer hospitality and you respond with gunfire."

"Come on out and we can talk," Fighting Devil said unctuously, guns ready.

"No way! I know your type. Before I appear I must guarantee my own safety."

"How?" Bill asked.

"Help!" the ornithopter expostulated. "I am trapped by a gravity field and cannot move."

"That's how. Without that frozen-down-flapper you are trapped on this mountain. And I don't have the switch with me to turn him loose. That is controlled by others who watch and listen to every word that we speak. Harm me and you harm yourselves, doom yourselves to eternity in these barren mountains. Ready to talk?"

"Yeah, yeah," Fighting Devil muttered as its weapons slipped out of sight.

With a crunching rumble a large boulder slid aside and from behind it emerged an incredibly battered machine. One side was bashed in and rusty, and it walked with a limp because it had a crudely carved and unbending metal leg in the place of the one that was missing. A black patch had been welded into lace over a blank eye socket and it leaned on a crutch made from crooked lengths of pipe.

"Welcome, visitors," it grated, "to Happy Acres. I am your host, Happy, and these are my acres."

Meta popped her eyes at it. "Happy? I don't think I want to see Unhappy Acres!"

"Yes, happy, as I will soon prove to you. We will go below and nourishment will be provided as soon as you lay down your weapons. Squishy creatures first, that's it, blasters on the ground."

"Moron!" Fighting Devil said with some feeling. "How can I lay down my weapons when they are all built in?"

"We have faced this problem before and have plenty of corks, plugs and safety wire. You will be secured. You may emerge now, dear comrades."

With a cacophony of rattles, creaks, clatters and thuds a band of even more beat-up creatures clanked into sight. It was a robot's nightmare—a junkdealer's dream. Some had treads missing from their tracks, limbs had been replaced by rusty prosthetics, bellybuttons by eggcups, eyeballs by lightbulbs; it was pretty revolting in a mechanical way.

"You guys don't look too good," Cy observed. "What's your problem?"

"All will be explained—but first—" Happy waved his helpers forward and they swarmed over the unhappy Fighting Devil. He had to be urged to produce his weapons which, reluctantly, he did, one by one. And as they emerged corks were hammered into gunbarrels, chambers plugged, lightning bolts grounded, fuses removed. Then his tentacles and arm extensions were wired together so he could not undo what had been done.

"Bombs too," Happy ordered. The orifice dilated in Fighting Devil's nether regions and the bombs plopped to the ground. Happy gave a rusty sigh of relief.

"It is always tricky when dealing with Fighting Devils. Some of them would rather die fighting than be disarmed . . ."

"I would rather die fighting!" Fighting Devil roared loudly—but it was too late. Solenoids clicked and buzzed while guns pointed futilely. However the broken brigade really knew their business and mayhem did not follow. Only a single small smoke grenade popped out of its kneecap and puffed into life.

"Follow me, dear guests," Happy said happily and led the way into the tunnel. Rusty, bent doors squeaked aside so they could pass, rumbled reluctantly shut behind them. The final portal admitted them to a high chamber that was feebly lit by dim bulbs that were festooned with metal spiders' webs. There was a long table in the center of the room. Sitting behind it were some more equally dilapidated machines.

"Welcome to PLDP," Happy intoned. "The acronym for our happy brotherhood. PLDP stands for the Planetary League of Deserters and Pacifists."

"If you will make that Interplanetary I'll join!" Bill said instantly.

"That is an interesting idea that might be well worth our consideration. What a joyful thought! Our movement could spread galaxy-wide, we could have a special branch for you squishies..."

"Traitors! Rebels!" Fighting Devil frothed and all its weapons popped out, writhed and trembled with suppressed rage, but all he managed to do was produce another smoke grenade.

"Stop that, will you!" Bill coughed, fanning at the smoke. "It doesn't help anything."

"Release me at once!" Fighting Devil thundered. "I will not hear these vilenesses spoken. A Fighting Devil does not belong here."

"That is what you say now," an ancient and crushed machine said from behind the table. "But we number more than one fighting devil in our ranks. You speak brazenly now, possessed of your strength, virility and phallic weapons—but you will talk out of the other side of your loudspeaker when your guns are spiked, your batteries discharged, your wad shot. Think! We were all like you once—now look at our state. My companion here, Grumpy, once commanded a legion of flame throwers. Right now he couldn't summon up enough spark to light a joint. Or dear Sleepy, the one dozing on the table, a permanent doze I fear for he hasn't moved for a month. Once he was a tank destroyer. Now he is destroyed himself and his tank is empty. Sic transit gloria machinery. For many of us it is too late. We came to PLDP when we were dis-

carded. We were rescued from the junkyard by bo-
dysnatchers, brought here in secrecy before we could
be recycled. But—I talk too much. You will be
hungry after your arduous journey. Pull up a hydraulic jack and tuck in. Rations will be taken to
your flying companion immobilized outside."

For all of his sneers Fighting Devil was not shy
about plunging his snout into a can of oil.

"You don't happen to have anything we can eat
—or drink?" Bill asked.

"By good fortune we do," Happy said, pointing
to a faucet on the wall. "Before we occupied these
premises they were used as a torture chamber. That
tap leads to—and I shudder to say it—a reservoir of
water. Be my guest. As to food, our scavengers sca-
venging the desert discovered alien objects adorned
with indecipherable script. Perhaps you can interpret
them," he said passing an alien object over.

Bill read the label and shuddered. "Yumee-
Gunge rations. The ones we threw away. Thanks a
lot, old buddy, but no thanks. But I will have a slug
of your torture juice."

"We may eat yet," Cy said, digging into his
pockets. "I think I got some of the seeds in here. I
picked the admiral's pockets." He produced a pink
plastic capsule.

"The color is different from the other ones,"
Meta said.

"So maybe the meat is different. Let's try it out."

Their hosts obliged them by pointing out a tunnel
that led to a sunlit cleft high on the side of the mountain. Windblown sand had collected here and a solitary
metal weed had taken root in this inhospitable soil.
They dampened the ground with water, pushed in the
seed and stepped back. Short instants later the crack-

ling plant had grown and the sizzling melon split open.

"Smells like ham," Bill said.

"Pig cells no doubt," Meta said as she carved off a slice. "If we had some mustard this would be paradise."

Replete, Bill leaned back against the sunwarmed rock and belched. "This is not too bad, you know. Maybe we ought to join up with PLDP and stay on here."

"We would starve to death since there isn't any food," Meta said with great practicality.

"And you would go through life with a great big yellow chicken foot at the end of your ankle," Cy observed with sadistic intent.

"That doesn't bother me," Bill said stretching his leg out in front of him and arching his toes. "It's not that bad once you get used to it."

"And great for scratching up worms!"

"Shut up, Cy," Meta said, "this is a serious conversation. There are some things that we must consider. If we desert now, our mission will have failed and this secret Chinger planetary base will never be discovered."

"So what?" Bill observed with impeccable logic. "What difference will it make? No one is ever going to win this war—or lose it. It is just going to go on forever. I have nothing against deserting and scratching out a precarious living with my chicken foot. But can we get away with it? There is plenty of food on the plateau. Maybe we can flap over there. We could trade with them. Send them junked machines so they won't have to shoot them down anymore."

"One thing that you are forgetting," Meta remembered. "We will be trapped here for the rest of our lives. No bright lights of the cities, theatre and posh restaurants afterward . . ."

"No foul wind off the bay replete with smells of decay and industrial waste blowing through the filthy streets of the Spunkk!" Cy chimed in with nostalgic longing. "No communal shoot-ups, orgies, juice-joints, reefers, rasters, suppositrods, rooster-boosters . . ."

"You're both mad," Bill huffed. "When was the last time you enjoyed any of those civilized pleasures? We are in the military and in it for life. We could make our home here, turn our backs on the mundane world, build log cabins, raise our children . . ."

"Knock off the male chauv crap! You are going to have me cooking and cleaning and wearing an apron next. No way! Since I am the only female person around here, and since I see that you want to enslave me in domesticity—I vote out. Sex for fun, that's my motto, and I got a lot to spare."

To prove her point she threw Bill to the ground, seized him in her tight embrace and gave him a soul kiss that raised his body temperature by seven degrees.

"May I take notes?" Fighting Devil said emerging from the tunnel. "To go with all my other notes about this bunch of commie traitors. I have carefully noted your talking about desertion, which I will report to your CO who will have you shot, or worse, for even considering it."

"Would you rat on your buddies?" Bill asked.

"Of course! I'm not called Fighting Devil for nothing, you know. The gods of war are my gods! Endless war stretches into the endless future and I marched forward into it triumphantly!"

It extruded its loudspeaker and began to play a hideous marching tune, stamped and strode around the ledge crying out war cries as it went.

"We have to get rid of this fruitcake before we talk about deserting again," Bill whispered.

"Bang on," Cy whispered back, then jumped to his feet and shouted, "You are so right, repellently warlike Fighting Devil! Your impeccable, logical arguments have convinced me. Reenlist! Fight on! Death to Chingers!"

"Death to Chingers!" Bill and Meta echoed and they all followed Fighting Devil around and around in a triumphant march until they dropped down exhausted.

"Weak fleshies," Fighting Devil exulted. "But at least you will fight now and there will be no more sniveling talk of desertion. We will march together into the future, into the sunset of eternal war. *Sieg heil!*"

It turned to face the sunset, arms and other appendages raised in salute, *sieg*ing and *heil*ing away like mad. Bill noticed that its toes were projecting over the edge. He tapped his companions on the shoulder, pointed and they nodded instant agreement. They all leaped to their feet, arms raised in victorious salute, marched forward with military precision to join Fighting Devil.

Then pushed it over the edge.

CHAPTER 17

AFTER A WHILE THE SPLINTERING AND CRASH-
ing sounds died away in the valley below.

"Scratch one Fighting Devil," Bill mused.

"Who will miss him?" Meta said as she started to
undress. "Time for a sunlit orgy, guys."

"On a full stomach?" Bill complained.

"On the hard rock! No way," Cy whined.

She sighed and rezipped. "Not only is romance
dead but so are your libidos. I got to find myself a
live one."

"I'm thirsty," Bill observed.

"The message is clear, numbnuts," she said disgustedly. "Back we go."

When they reentered the central hall the meeting
was just ending. There were rusty cheers and creaking salutes at the conclusion. Happy rattled forward
and welcomed them effusively.

"Dear soft, unmetallic companions, the vote has
been taken. We offer you refuge—and we will make
plans at once to open a squishy section of the PLDP.
We are filled with elation at the thought. Our simple
movement will now spread to the stars. We will
carry the word to all the planets—speak, convert
and convince. Entire armies will desert at our behest,
great fleets will grow silent and dark as their crews

164

rally to our noble cause. The bright future begins. Peace in our time! In our metallic hands we hold the future! The end to all war..."

It broke off the inspiring speech as the creaking door creaked open and a squad of machines with red metal crosses welded to their chests stamped in. They staggered under the weight of a stretcher that bore the badly crunched form of a Fighting Devil. But this devil would fight no more. It looked like it had come through the wars. Its right leg had been torn off and replaced with one of its cannons. Most of its weaponry was broken or missing and it wore dark glasses over its crunched optics.

"Another victim of the endless wars," Happy observed. "How tragic. Welcome to the PLDP, no longer fighting Fighting Devil. Your travails are at an end and you have found safe harbor at last. Is there anything you would like to say in greeting?"

The fractured Fighting Devil lifted one trembling arm and pointed a bent and broken finger at the humans present.

"J'accuse!" it grated.

"I thought it looked a little familiar," Bill mused, then continued brightly. "Why say, if that isn't our old friend Fighting Devil itself. Had a little trouble? No, don't talk about it, we'll all feel too depressed. Just let me be the first to welcome you to the ranks of the PLDP and a long and happy retirement."

"Let me be second. Welcome," Meta smiled.

"Third. Welcome..."

"You did it!" Fighting Devil screeched mechanically, then dropped back onto the stretcher. "Cut down in my youth. Pushed off the cliff by squishies. What an ignoble end to a Fighting Devil in its prime.

To end my days here, among all these wrecks. A wreck myself...It is too awful to contemplate. If I had a working weapon left I would blow myself away. No, not yet! Justice must be done first. They did it! The soft-ploppies who stand guiltily before you. They pushed me off the cliff and must be made to pay for their crime. Shoot them down! Kill them while I laugh, ha-ha, at their deserved fate..."

It dribbled oil incontinently as Happy, no longer happy, turned to face his human guests.

"Has this poor creature's brain been addled by falling a mile down the mountain—or is there any truth in what it says?"

"Traumatic hallucinations," Cy observed. "It tripped, started to fall. We tried to save it, but could not. The end of a Fighting Devil is always a tragedy. We should pity it..."

"I have...recordings sealed in armor. I can prove what...you did."

Cy's unctuous smile was replaced by a snarl that cut his face like a knife slash in a corpse's belly. "Are you going to believe this battered metal bastard—or us?"

"It—if it has proof," Happy decided. "Put up or shut up, recently crunched Fighting Devil."

"How's about...that!" It rasped exultantly as a projector with a cracked lens clattered out of its right hip. The image projected on the wall was jumpy and out of focus. But it was clear enough to see that the humans had pushed it off the cliff. Then the projector vibrated violently and fell to the floor. But the damage had been done. All eyes—that were able to operate—were on the humans.

Bill rushed to their defense. "Make it tell you why we did it. We had good reason—it was going to turn us in, have us tried and shot for desertion. We acted merely in self-defense. The kind of pre-emptive strike that the military is always jawing about. What else could we have done?"

"Many things. But what is done is done," Happy said. "You are guilty as charged."

"Shoot them!" Fighting Devil grated obscenely.

The humans fell back before the advancing metallic hordes, sweeping the room with the eyes of a trapped animal. (This was very hard on the trapped animal.) But there was no escape. Closer they came and closer, rusty claws reached out, bent mandibles clattered for justice. They were back to the wall now, the first vengeful metal hands closed on them. One zipped down Bill's fly. . .

"Stop!" Happy shouted with lungs of steel. "Back, back I say. Two wrongs do not make a right. Aren't you all forgetting the name of our organization? PLDP. And what does that stand for?"

The massed voices of the machines boomed out.

"Planetary League of Deserters and Pacifists."

"And what is our anthem?"

"They who fight and get away, will not fight another day!"

"Second chorus."

"We will turn the other cheek, fight no more though our oil leak!"

"That's how the file files," Happy said gloomily. "As much as we would like to rend you asunder, separate cog from wheel, nut from bolt, we cannot. Our philosophy forbids it. You will be turned out of this sanctuary, returned to the military from whence you fled, which should be punishment enough."

"Would you guys take a harmless recording

back for my dear commander Zots?" Fighting Devil asked insincerely.

They all gave him the finger, knowing full well what recording he would send.

"Go!" Happy ordered. "You are banned, purged, rejected. Leave and take our bad wishes with you."

"Could we take our blasters, too?" Cy suggested.

Gears grated angrily deep within Happy's gut. "You try my patience sorely. If I don't see your cans out of here in the next ten seconds I am going to reconsider my decision."

"That was a close one," Bill said as they climbed back up the tunnel to freedom.

"Quiet!" Cy cozened. "Not a word about this to the ornithopter. Tell him that Fighting Devil decided to stay here, or some other big lie. We are lost if he suspects."

The ornithopter spat out a mouthful of rusty metal that it was chewing on and turned an eye in their direction.

"Just got a radio message from Fighting Devil. Says to turn you in when we get back for knocking him off."

"We cannot lie about it, although we would like to," Meta said. "Going to rat on us?"

"Hell, no. I don't like this war any more than you do. They got my sister and most of my relatives. We stick to our story. We all say how great the others did their job, then ask for a furlough."

"What about Fighting Devil?" Bill asked.

"That intrepid, loyal, Fighting Devil!" the ornithopter said, eyes spinning passionately in their sockets. "Though the vile Barthroomians attacked in their thousands, millions, it still fought on. Fighting until the very last volt in its batteries was discharged to enable us to escape. Giving up its own life that we might be saved."

"You don't fly very well," Meta said admiringly, "but you are one great fiction writer."

"Why thank you. I have sold a few things, but only to the little magazines. And I would fly a hell of a lot better if I had a propeller—flapping wings consume too much energy to provide lift. Having said that—let's flap off before anything else happens. I've got a date with an ornithopterette with nest-eggs in mind."

They suffered the rattling ride in silence. Not really wanting to go back, but seeing no alternative. The ornithopter, refreshed by rest and repast, made good time of it. Soon the metal city hauled itself over the horizon, which is hard to do, and they soared down among the soaring towers. The admiral and Wurber came out as they were clambering weakly to the platform.

"About time you got back," Praktis welcomed them graciously. "I want you to file complete reports and have them on my desk before 0700. Then I need a volunteer." He snarled as they all shuffled backwards, stopping only with their backs to the wall. In more ways than one.

"Cowards! And you don't even know what it is yet."

"Nothing good—or you wouldn't have thought of it," Cy said, speaking for all of them.

"Smartass. I need a volunteer to penetrate the enemy's stronghold, to then find the Chinger spaceship. Then to enter it and use the FTL communicator to send a message to the Space Navy to rescue us."

"Is that all?" Meta asked, her voice dripping with sarcasm. She wiped it off her chin.

"Yes, that's all. And someone had better think of a way to do it fast. Wurber and I ate the last melonsteak yesterday. So prepare to starve—or leave. My research is done so I have no reason to stay. In fact I look forward to returning to the luxuries and comforts of military life."

"Only for officers," Cy growled.

"Of course! Now—let's have some suggestions!"

The silence that followed was broken by a voice they had not heard in a long time. "I know how it can be done."

It was Captain Bly. Red-eyed, trembling—but sober and unstoned.

"Since when are you offering help," Praktis said with dark suspicion.

"Since I ran out of dope. I need a new supply."

"Now that I believe. What's your plan?"

"Simple. We kill them all. Every metal traitor, every Chinger. Boom. Dead."

"That's simple, all right," Praktis sneered. "About as simple and stupid an idea I have ever heard."

"Go ahead and sneer! I have been sneered at for years. Yes, and laughed at too. Derided and rejected, and I have even had nightpots emptied on my head. Ohh, if only I hadn't had the dog in bed too . . ."

"Captain, your plan, what is it?"

Meta's voice penetrated the fog of his whining and self-indulgent pity so that he blinked and looked about.

"Plan? What plan? Oh, yes. Killing them all in the mountain stronghold. We drop a neutron bomb on them. As is common knowledge this kills all forms of life—but does not harm property. Then we just walk in and grab their spacer."

"Simplicity itself," Praktis said, pointing to his lips. "And I hope you will notice that I am still sneering. We don't have a neutron bomb, bowbhead, do we?"

"No we don't. But before I became a garbage tug captain I was a nuclear physicist. All of that before the dog incident, of course. And there is plenty of neutronium in the engines of the wrecked garbage tug."

"All burnt up now," Bill said.

"Just because you look stupid don't act stupid too. The neutronium is sealed in and armor plated. It's still there."

"I think, Cap, that you are onto something good," Praktis said, eyes gleaming with murderous intent. "We go to the ship, extract the neutronium, build a bomb, drop it and get the spacer. Wonderful!"

"No go," Zots said, waving a languid golden arm. The carriers carried him around the landing strip a few times then gently sat his palanquin down. "The bombing deal is off."

"Why?" Praktis asked, puzzled.

"Why? Because it would end the endless war for one thing."

"But you want that?"

"I do not. Nor does my brother Plotz who is in charge of the insane machines. Who all of them, PS, think that we are the insane machines."

"Speaking of insane machines..." Meta did not

finish the sentence but jerked her thumb in Zots's direction.

"Just watch that," Zots grated, a scowl marking his usual golden expression. "The whole thing is a put-up job if you must know. Plotz and I lust after power—and we got it in plenty since we started this war. It keeps the economy turning over, provides plenty of junk metal so we never go hungry. Lots of good comes out of it."

"Lots of destruction, maiming, death comes out of it," Bill said.

"That too. So what's new? You humans are up to the same game, aren't you, Admiral?"

"More or less. So keep your war, that's your problem. Our problem is getting off this planet before we starve to death. What about that?"

"You just said it—it's your problem."

"You're all heart. Do you expect us just to stay here and starve to death?"

"That's it. You got it right without any help."

"You tinkertoy traitor!" Praktis howled with fury. He rushed to the attack as did all the others. The attack stopped instantly when ten Fighting Devils ran out of the tunnel entrance and formed a protective screen.

"You'll not get away with this," Praktis frothed. "We will tell every machine about this fake war. Hear that, Fighting Devils, carrybots? The whole war is a fake. You die for nothing."

"You speak for nothing," Zots yawned boredly. "I issued the command by radio to all my troops to forget your language. They can no longer understand you."

Bill looked up at their faithful steed, the virile

ornithopter. An eye swiveled in his direction as he spoke.

"It's not true, what he said. You understand me, don't you?"

"*Comment?*"

"You can't have forgotten how to speak with us—not that quickly!"

"*Enfin, des tables de monnaies et de mesures rendront de réels services.*"

"You've forgotten that quickly."

Then he turned back and saw that Zots and his entourage were gone, the Fighting Devils as well. A great flapping sounded and died away as the ornithopter took off.

They stared at each other with horrified gazes.

Alone.

Trapped on this barren world.

To starve to death. Was this their fate?

CHAPTER **18**

"I CAN'T BELIEVE THIS IS HAPPENING TO ME!"
Cy moaned whimpily.

"Well it ain't happening to the man in the
moon!" Meta snarled. "We will all feel sorry for ourselves later. Right now we have got to make a plan."

"So make," Praktis gloomed. "I'm open to all
suggestions, no matter how wild."

His answer was only silence. After a long time
Bill coughed. "I'm thirsty. I'm going to get a drink
of water. Can I bring any back for anybody? One
thing we know, there's plenty of water so we don't
die of thirst."

He retreated under the barrage of their insults,
pausing at the tunnel entrance only to catch his
breath. Before he could go on Meta called out to
him.

"Bill, hold it. There's a dragon here that wants
to talk to you."

It had made a perfect four-point landing and
now sat peacefully, puffing the occasional smoke
ring.

"Hi there, Bill, and all you folks. I had a good
flight. As you see I came to join you here as soon as
the wing grew back. I couldn't return to dragon-
hold, not after turning traitor. So I thought you

might have a job for me in this neck of the woods."

"We sure do!" they all exulted. "You are going to get us out of here."

"No problem. But I'll need to refill my tank first. A barrel or two of oil should do."

"That could be a problem," Praktis said. "We have had a difference of opinion with the locals."

"So we don't talk to them," Captain Bly said. "There's a supply room just down this corridor. I suggest that you and you volunteer to roll out the barrel."

"It's always the enlisted men who get the dirty work," Bill muttered petulantly.

"And the enlisted girls too," Meta said. "So instead of feeling sorry for ourselves shall we just go and do the job?"

The door to the supply room was open, but a small inventorybot was taking inventory. Keeping track on a wax tablet with a metal stylo. They brushed past it and pushed over two of the full barrels and started to roll them from the room. The inventorybot blocked the doorway and waved its fourteen arms furiously.

"XII, II, XVI, VIX!" it said.

"Sure, sure," Bill agreed. "But you got a whole room full. You're not going to miss two little ones."

"XXIXIIXXX!" it screamed at them.

It crunched when they rolled the barrels over it. But it must have got off a final radio call because before they could get back to the landing strip Zots came hurrying up on his palanquin.

"Did you just run down my inventorybot?"

"It was an accident, it tripped right in front of the barrel."

"Am I supposed to believe that old crapola?"

" 'Tis but the truth," Bill said, placing his hand over his heart and looking saintly.

"Thousands would believe you—but I don't. And what were you doing with the oil anyway?"

Bill was all lied out but Meta rose to the occasion. "You want us to die," she sobbed. "No food. Starve to death. So we thought maybe we would sip a little oil, get used to it, it is filled with rich hydrocarbons after all—and we are carbon based life forms. Would you begrudge dying aliens a last sip of oil?"

"All right, all right, enough already. I got more important things to do than to jaw-jaw with squishies. There's a war on you know."

The palanquin vanished down the corridor and Bill let out a woosh of relief. "You were marvelous!" he said, spaniel eyes gleaming moistly at Meta.

"Wasn't I though. I have real acting talents. I'm more than just another pretty face you know. Or do you know? I seem to be getting very little feedback from you. You are interested, aren't you? Or are you kinky or bent, Bill? Let me know now so I won't go on wasting my time. Who do you find more attractive—me or Cy?"

"You, of course! What do you think I am?"

"Just checking up. Now put your mouth where your money is!"

She grabbed him in a warm embrace and they kissed. Her mouth was a passionate tiger longing to consume him—

"Ouch! You bit me!"

"Love play, toots—and it gets better..."

"You two. Knock off the heterosexuality on duty. Get those barrels rolling."

Praktis watched suspiciously as they rolled past,

then followed them out onto the landing strip.

"How delightful!" the dragon flared appreciatively. "Vintage Pennzoil. Delicious."

It holed a barrel with a quick stab of one steel claw, upended and drained it in one dragonian chugalug. Then belched flame appreciatively and covered them all with a cloud of soot.

"I do apologize for my table manners." Its voice died to a liquid mumble as it drank the second barrel as well. Then the air was filled with a loud crunching and clanking as it ate the barrels.

"Can we talk now?" Praktis said when the last morsel of steel had slipped from sight.

"Surely. You want transportation?"

"Correct."

"Where to?"

"Good question," Praktis mused. "You might take us back to the plateau that you all enjoyed visiting so much. You said that the food there was edible."

"But the autochthons are not!" Cy complained, and the others nodded complete agreement. "A bunch of crazies. And there is no future there with everybody just chasing around, killing each other."

"A well-made point. Where else then? We can't surrender to the Chingers."

"Why not?" They all turned to look at Bill with various expressions of revulsion; Cy bent and picked up a large rock. "Now wait a minute! We're just looking at possibilities. There aren't that many choices, you know. The Chingers say that they are peaceful and don't like to kill or make war. So make them prove it. We go there. They have to feed us or we croak. If they don't have food we can eat—then they have to get us offplanet soonest."

"That plan is so stupid it might work," Captain Bly said hoarsely through his cottonmouth.

"I say no—and I'm the admiral. No surrender. Except as a last resort. Is there any place else we can go on this desert planet?"

"Well," the dragon said. All eyes were on him. He brushed them off. "I remember a story this old dragon used to tell when we sat around the fire at night roasting nuts. And bolts. He spoke of the green plateau we have just visited, and of the repulsive life forms that infest it. But he talked as well of another plateau, also of the same hideous shade of green, that lies almost a day's flight beyond the first one. But he warned us not to go near it. For Great Dangers lurked there. And Evil as well."

"He said that? Great Dangers and Evil?"

"Yup. Just like that. And if you think it easy to speak in capital letters just try it some time."

"No thank you," Praktis said. "I would like to make sure of just one detail. You did say it was green?"

"Green as a dragon's eye in heat."

"An interesting simile. Great. We go."

"What about all the Great Dangers and Evil?" Bill complained. "That doesn't sound good."

"What does? Just follow orders, trooper. The first order is to shut up. All right, we leave at once. It is going to be a bumpy flight—so everyone who hasn't gone, go now. I don't want to make any pit stops. Tally-ho!"

Just as they were climbing aboard, a familiarly repulsive voice called out. "That dragon! I want to talk to you."

The palanquin trotters had trotted out the palanquin with Zots aboard.

"Yes, sir," the dragon said, looking back to see if the passengers were safely aboard.

"Shake those alien squishies off at once—that is an order. I don't like any of this."

"Oh, sir, I hope that you like this better."

With that the dragon breathed a blast of flame that melted the trotters and the palanquin instantly. Only Zots, being goldplated, survived. He shrieked warmly and ran to safety as the dragon fired up its boilers.

"Up, up and away!" it yodeled and hurled itself into the air.

"We're ever so grateful for your aid," Meta said gratefully.

"Think nothing of it. Ever since I left the egg I have been taught to hate Zots and his lotz. He might be a nice fellow. . ."

"He's a metallic meathead!"

"Good. One enjoys having one's prejudices proved correct. So—lovely flying weather. Next stop the Plateau of Mystery."

"And give the other plateau a wide miss," Bill cozened. "Remember what happened last time."

"How could I forget. The new wing still isn't broken in right."

Fueled by the high octane oil, the dragon flew all night. No one slept, particularly the dragon, for obvious reasons, and it was a bleary-eyed bunch that greeted the rising sun. They blinked into its brightness and there—dead ahead—a plateau rose from the desert wastes.

"We've made it," Bill said hoarsely.

"Not quite," the dragon said, yawning out a little fireball. "I'm going to get some altitude in case they are trigger-happy down there as well."

They soared in circles, riding the updrafts, before the dragon ventured inland.

"Smoking volcanoes," Praktis said. "Stay away from them."

"For the moment, if you insist. But I do love lava! Lambent licking flame, fuming fumaroles. My kind of stuff. And that looks like your kind of stuff down there. Is that a war going on?"

Praktis lifted his eyepatch and his telescopic eyelens whirred out. "Very interesting. There appears to be large structure of some sort, a castle it looks like. Heavily defended because it is being heavily attacked. Details not too clear from this height, but it looks like a standoff. Take us down, dragon."

"Not to the war," Bill wailed.

"No, dummy, not to the war. But close to it. There, mighty steed, do you see that tree-covered hill? Set down on the other side, out of sight of the attackers. We can reconnoiter from there."

With their limbs paralyzed from the long flight they could only slide to the ground and lie there kicking feebly like turned-over beetles.

"Hope you enjoyed the trip," the dragon said.

"Great. Wonderful. Whee." They gasped.

"That's nice. I'm going to leave you here because warring squishies are not my bag. See you around."

They waved feebly as powerful wings hurled their fiery charger into the air. He roared his farewells and a thin shower of soot descended upon their limp forms.

Bill was the first to stir, standing and groaning with the effort. They were in a grassy glade across which a merry brook bubbled.

"I'm going to get a drink from that merry brook," he said and staggered off.

As soon as they were able the others joined him and they all stretched out on the bank slurping and gulping like crazy. Restored, they were soon sitting up and examining their new home. Birds sang, bees hummed, flowers dipped saucy blossoms in the breeze and the admiral barked commands.

"You, Second Lieutenant. Take a shufty at the other side of the hill and report back soonest. The rest of you scour the landscape for fruit, berries, anything to eat. And remember, eating yourself is a court-martial offense. All food to be brought to me for evaluation."

"Some chance," Meta muttered malignantly and the rest of them nodded agreement. They spread out as Bill worked his way up the hill through the brush, until he could see what was happening on the other side. He sheltered under a bush, which just happened to be a blackberry bush, so he really enjoyed himself, watching and munching. When he had eaten his fill he took one last berry, for the admiral, and went back down the hill.

The others had returned before him and the admiral was bitching them out. "One piece of fruit each you brought back! Do you take me for a dummy? Don't answer that. And what about you, Lieutenant, what have you got?"

"A berry!" He handed it over and Praktis frothed angrily.

"A berry! And your face shmeared blue." He glared, but he still popped it into his mouth and munched it. "Report. What's happening over there?"

"It's like this, sir." He burped purple and the admiral's glare got turned up a couple more notches.

"That castle we spotted on the way down, it's completely surrounded by the attackers from what I could see. The drawbridge is up and every once in a while they pour some boiling oil on the army below. There is a lot of shouting and rushing about, but they don't seem to be in any hurry."

"What kind of guns are they using?"

"That's the funny part. They don't have any guns. There are big wooden machines that throw rocks, other kinds that shoot out long spears. The troops are armed with spears, as well as bows and arrows and swords, that kind of thing. And, at first, I thought the attackers were all women because they were wearing skirts. Then when I got closer I saw that they had really hairy legs and were all men . . ."

"Just save your perverted sexual observations for your barracks mates. Did you see any food?"

"Did I!" Bill's eyes glowed with passion. "They had a fire going with a carcass roasting on a spit over it. I could smell the cooking meat real good."

They all swallowed and spat and coughed as the saliva rushed to their mouths.

"We have to make contact," Praktis said. "And for this we need a volunteer."

CHAPTER 19

"ADMIRAL PRAKTIS," META SAID SWEETLY, "I think that it is time that we got one thing straight."

She made a fist, strolled over—and popped him in the eye. He sprawled out on the greensward with the shiner already beginning to shine greenly.

"You struck me!"

"You noticed?"

"Troops!" he frothed, saliva buds flying in all directions. "Mutiny! Kill this traitor at once!"

There was no rush to justice. In fact only Cy moved, yawning as he strolled over and kicked Praktis in the ribs.

"Are you getting the message?" Captain Bly asked grotesquely. "Seeing the incomprehension lurking behind your glazed eyeballs, I had better spell it out. We are countless light years from our nearest base—which doesn't even know where we are. Our chances of leaving this planet are very slim indeed. So it looks like, as long as we are here, that all rank is suspended for the duration. We will address each other by our first names. Mine is Archibald."

"I like Captain better," Meta said. "What's your first name, Praktis?"

"Admiral," he snarled bitterly.

"Fine, if that's the way you want it. But no more orders or pulling rank or any of that military bowb, hear?"

"I will never submit to the rule of the proletariat!"

They all began kicking him in the ribs until he cried out, "Long Live the Peoples' Socialist Republic of Usa!"

"That's more like it," Cy said. "So what do we do next?"

"Make a plan?" Bill said brightly.

"Shut up," Praktis implied. "I am permitted to talk, aren't I, now that I am just one of the gang?"

"One man, one vote. Speak."

"There is a war going on here. And there is an army out there. During a war when the army is around it is the civilians who suffer. Okay so far?"

"Your chains of logic are impeccable."

"Then we don't act like civilians. We do the military shtick and join the army. And get fed. I suggest that we organize a military unit, *elect* a commanding officer. Then go volunteer."

"Any ideas who should be CO?" Bill asked.

"Probably the ex-admiral," Meta said. "What with the black monocle, balding head and obnoxious manners he looks like officer material. Also he has had experience of command in a former life. You want the job, Praktis?"

"I never thought you would ask," he smarmed in dulcet tones. His voice changed and he snarled the command. "Fall in!" Then sweetly, "Please. That is very cooperative of you. We've got to make this look good, so try to keep in step if you can possibly manage it. Backs arched, chins sucked in, chests out —forward HAARCH!"

He put the little loudspeaker on his shoulder and played the inspiring march, "Rumble of Rockets, Roar of Cannon, Screams of the Dying," which has a very large bass drum beat so even the dumbest of dummies knows when to come down with the left foot.

Through the meadow they marched and around the hill towards the attacking army. When they marched into sight the battle slowed and ground to a stop as popping eyes and gaping jaws turned their way. The officer who appeared to be directing the operation, dressed in brass and leather armor, turned in their direction as well. The sound of their singing drowned out even the drip-drip of the boiling oil from the castle above. They roared the words into the echoing sky.

> "When you hear the rockets rumble,
>   And the cannons' roaring din,
>   You can bet that all the troopers
>   Have sent their box-tops in!"

It was a very military display, as long as you didn't know very much about military display. They thudded and marched their way over to the officer and Praktis screamed one last command.

"Company, HAA-LT!"

They stamped to a stop before the officer and Praktis snapped a far snappier salute than was his normal practice.

"All present and accounted for, SIR. Admiral Praktis and his company reporting for duty, SIR."

The officer first looked plused, then nonplused, at their sudden appearance. He turned and barked a hoarse command over his shoulder. An elderly man in a filthy robe, sporting an equally filthy white beard, tottered up to face them.

"*Ave atque vale?*" the elderly creature quavered.

"Beats me, Pops," Praktis answered. "I speak the odd language or two but never heard of this one."

The oldster cocked his hand behind his ear, listened and nodded his head. Turned to the officer.

"A barbaric mixture of Gaelic tongues, Centurion. A little Anglo, a little Saxon, a guttural drop or two of Old Norse—plus the odd bit of Latin. Pretty boring and not an inflected noun in sight."

"No lectures, Stercus. You're just a slave around here. Back to work cooking the ox and I'll take over this operation." He looked Praktis and his little band up and down and scowled cruelly. "And just what in the name of Great Jupiter do we have here?"

"Volunteers, noble Centurion. Mercenary soldiers willing to serve in your ranks."

"Where are your weapons?"

"There was a small difficulty..."

"What was it?"

The admiral had no ready lies available, but Meta, who was getting plenty of practice, rose to the occasion.

"It is a matter of honor and our good commander does not want to speak of it. But a short time ago we were caught in a sudden flash flood while crossing a stream. In order not to drown we had to discard our weapons and swim for our lives. Of course for a soldier to lose his or her weapons is a great dishonor and our commander tried to throw himself onto his sword, but of course his sword was gone. So he led us here to enlist and restore our lost honor in the battle's clash..."

"All right—enough is enough!" the Centurion shouted, wondering if blood was coming out of his ears. "A short, succinct explanation is adequate. In any case I don't believe a word of it." He saw that Meta was starting to speak again and he shouted aloud. "Desist! I believe you, I believe you. And it just so happens I could use some more troops. Pay is one sesterce a day. You will be issued one sword and one shield each and your salaries will be stopped until they are paid for. Which will take about a year, or until you are killed, whichever comes first. Your weapons, being the property of the state, will revert to the state should this occur . . ."

"We agree to the terms of enlistment," Praktis shouted, drowning out the military waffle. "We are in your service and when do we eat?"

"Ox coming off the fire now!" the elderly slave shouted and the newcomers almost got trampled in the rush. But not quite, since they had all been on plenty of chowlines before. Quick work with the elbows and a karate chop or two saw to it that their brave little band was head of the queue when the food was served out. They escaped the starving stampede and carried their sizzling booty to a nearby grove where they noshed it down.

"That," Cy said, "was fatty, raw, overcooked, gristly and generally repulsive. But good." They nodded agreement and rubbed the grease from their fingers onto the grass. "What do we wash it down with?"

Bill pointed. "There is a barrel over there and soldiers lining up with cups."

They joined the line and grabbed cups from the pile. They were made of leather and appeared to be coated with tar. Privilege of rank, Praktis went first and held out the cup for the liquid to be ladled into it. He drank deep then sprayed out the mouthful.

"Akkkh! This wine tastes like vinegar and water."

"That's because it is vinegar and water," the KP said. "Wine only for officers. Next."

"But I am an officer!"

"Take it up with the union—not my problem. Next."

Foul as it was, it at least washed down the even fouler meat. They drained the cups and dropped to the grass for a postprandial snooze. Praktis stirred in his sleep as the sun left his face and a shadow fell over him. He opened one eye to see the dark figure standing before him.

"To arms!" he cried and groped around for his sword.

"'Tis but I, Stercus the slave," Stercus the slave said. "You are the admiral who is in charge of this unit?"

Praktis sat up suspiciously. "Yeah. Who wants to know?"

"Stercus the Slave..."

"We've already had the introductions. What's up?"

"Is an admiral an officer?"

"Highest in the navy."

"What is a navy?"

"Is there any point to all of this?"

"Yes, sir."

"In the navy you say aye aye, sir."

"Aye aye, sir."

"That's better. What's up?"

"This is the most boring and stupid conversation I have heard in my entire life," Meta said, lying back down and pulling her jacket over her head.

"Wine is for officers," Stercus said, swinging a bulging skin bottle off his back. "Since you are an officer I have brought you some."

"I am beginning to like this army," Praktis enthused, raising the wineskin and shooting a dark jet down his throat.

After being pounded on the back for about five minutes he stopped coughing. They were all awake by this time and Bill tried a bit of wine, a small amount, and his eyes bulged.

"I've tasted worse. I think," he said hoarsely.

"But it contains alcohol," Praktis said, even more hoarsely. "Pass it back."

"May a poor slave ask what brings you warriors to these parts," Stercus asked coyly, seeing that they were all well on the way to getting bombed out of their minds.

"So that's why you are here," Cy said. "Sent by your officer to spy on us. Deny that?"

"Why should I," the old man cackled. "It's true. He wants to know where you come from and what you are doing here."

They all looked at Meta who seemed to have been appointed Liar's Mate First Class.

"We come from a far distant land . . ."

"Can't be too far, this plateau isn't that big."

She smiled and shifted gears on the lie-machine. "I did not say that we were from this plateau. We are from the other plateau and we fled here across the trackless sands of the endless desert, fleeing the endless war there."

"You are not the first to seek escape from meshugana Barthroomians. But since you are neither red nor green Barthroomians you must be hideous great white apes."

"Has that rumor spread this far? Just forget the ape crap. A lot goes on over there that you don't know about."

"Nor do I care. I'm just trying to get you drunk to find out where you hid your radium rifles."

"We didn't bring any."

"You sure? Last chance."

"We're sure. Now we have the wine, for what it is worth, Stercus. So just push off. If we had any other weapons do you think that we would enlist in this two-bit army?"

The old slave stroked his beard and bobbed his head. "Now that, admiral, has the ring of truth to it. So, with no other weapons, you are willing to fight armed only with sword and shield or primitive fighting apparatus."

"That's it."

"And that's all I wanted to know. Enjoy the wine." He bobbed his head in slavely humility and they waved condescendingly in his direction.

Stercus raised the little whistle that he had concealed in the palm of his hand and blew a shrill blast. Soldiers burst from the trees on all sides and in an instant they had myriad sharp spears pointed to their throats.

"Bring them along," Stercus ordered. "We've got six new volunteers for the circus."

"Dancing bears, clowns and elephants?" Bill asked happily.

"Spears, swords, nets, tridents, lions, tigers—and certain death!" the aged slave cackled chastely.

CHAPTER **20**

AT SPEARPOINT THE BRAVE LITTLE BAND WAS
driven through the camp, to the jeers and rude cries
of the rough soldiers.

"You'll be sorry!"

"Morituri te salutamus!"

"Foreigners!"

"Barbarians!"

"Poofters!"

Ignoring the insults, most of which they could
not understand anyway, they marched on to the
Centurion's tent.

"Hail, Centurion Pediculus, hail!" the ancient
slave hailed in a cackling gasp. "The prisoners are
here."

Pediculus pushed aside the tentflap and
emerged. He had stripped off his armor and donned
a loose tunic to better reveal his manly form. He had
a potbelly, knock-knees and cross-eyes. "Parade
them before me," he ordered looking at everyone
and no one at the same time.

Swords and spears convinced the prisoners to
line up while Pediculus inspected them.

"A handsome big burly fangy chap," he said,
looking at Bill.

"Oh, thank you, sir!" he smarmed.

"Start off with him. He should go few rounds before he's killed."

"I'll kill you first, Tubby!"

Bill growled and leapt forward—but was kept from his prey by the drawn swords. Pediculus smiled sadistically which made his false teeth protrude and he pushed them back in slurpily. He eyed the admiral, Cy, Wurber and Bly with disdain as he strolled past—until he came to Meta where his eyes trembled to a focus on her fulsome form.

"Take the others to the arena," he ordered. "Except for this one! Strip her and anoint her with balsam and myrrh and lemon scented washing up liquid. Then drape her in the finest silk and she shall be my love slave."

"Oh, thank you, kind commander!" Meta breathed, seizing his hand and bending to kiss it. "You're kind of cute, in a paleonihilistic way. And that's the most romantic offer I have had in years. I would swoon at this sublime opportunity if your teeth fitted better."

Even as she spoke she seized his hand and in an expert movement seized his elbow as well, twisted and pulled. Pediculus screamed in agony—then in fear as she whirled him into the air then threw him against his tent. Which collapsed and enveloped him. Soldiers hurried forward in response to his muffled roars of pain. Neither Meta, nor the others, moved as sharp swordpoints quivered at their throats.

"Nice," Bill said. "You're a girl in a million!"

"Thanks, toots, a kind word always appreciated. I was also judo champion three years running of LAGTAA."

"Lactate?"

"No, cretin, LAGTAA. That is the Lifeboat and Garbage Tug Athletic Association."

"To the arena!" Pediculus screeched, being helped from the remains of the tent. He had lost his teeth and his wig hung over his eyes. "Death, blood, destruction—I can hardly wait! And that muscle-bound doxie goes first."

Swept forward at spearpoint, followed by the roaring mob of soldiers, they were driven to the arena. It was a natural glade that had been terraced in a half circle to face the leveled and walled patch of blood-stained ground below. This was lined with cages and the prisoners were pushed into the nearest one. There was a fierce howling from the adjoining cage and they all drew back lest they be mauled through the bars. All except Meta who put her hand through the bars before they could stop her.

"Here, kitty-kitty," she said. The sinister look-ing tomcat mewed happily as she scratched its head. It was a one-eyed, scarred and tough alley fighter.

"But only about two feet long," Bill said.

"And it's the only animal in sight," Cy added, pointing to the other cages. "All empty. What hap-pened to the lions, and tigers?"

"It's the wrong season for them," the slave-master said as he stalked up, cracking his whip. "We only have lions and tigers when there is an X in the month."

"There are no months with X's in them," Praktis said pedantically.

"Yeah? What about XII and XI, wise guy. All right, the fun begins. I need a volunteer to go first."

When the dust settled they were all pressed against the back of the cage. Praktis and Captain Bly were last since they didn't have the enlisted troops' instant reflex to the word *volunteer*. The slave-master chuckled sadistically.

"No volunteers? Then I'll pick one myself. You, big boy, the Centurion wants you to lead off the prelims. He's saving the tootsie for the main event."

"Good luck, Bill," they called out, pushing him forward. "You die fighting for a noble cause."

"It's been nice knowing you, big fellow. Happy journey."

"May you be in heaven for an hour before the devil knows you're dead."

"Gee, thanks, guys. That's a big help."

Bill was horribly depressed by the entire affair. War and all its terrors was one thing. But a screwball and deadly circus on this lost plateau? He could not believe that it was happening to him.

"It's happening to you all right," the slave-master gurgled antipathetically. "Now take this sword and net and get out there and put on a good show. Or else."

"Or else what? What could be worse than this?" He hefted the weight of the sword and got a good grip on it as his muscles tensed.

"What could be worse? You could be drawn, quartered, flayed, boiled in oil, have your fingernails pulled out for openers."

Roaring with rage Bill hurtled forward. And stopped when he saw the ranked bowmen, arrows pulled back, all aiming at him.

"Message clear?" the slave-master asked. "Now go forth and remember your orders.

Bill looked up at the massed, screaming soldiers, the royal box occupied by harlots and Pediculus's sadistic, pot-bellied form. There didn't seem to be much choice. He turned and shuffled out into the arena swishing the sword and swinging the net and wondering how the hell he had ever gotten into this mess. He was alone in the arena—but a cage on the far side was being opened and from the gate stepped a tall, blond-haired man carrying a trident. His fine garments were torn and his fine boots scuffed. Yet he strode forward like a king, seemingly ignorant of the roaring rabble. He stamped up and stopped before Bill, eyeing him up and down.

"Well, varlet," he spake. "What hite ye."

"About six feet two in my stocking feet."

"Methinks thee mithunderstood. What be your name and rank?"

"Bill, trooper, Temporary Acting Second Lieutenant."

"I am Arthur, King of Avalon—though these varlets know it not. You may call me Art to preserve this secret."

"OK, Art. My friends call me Bill."

This exchange of conversation rather than assassination had infuriated the mob who hurled epithets and empty bottles into the arena.

"We must battle, friend Bill—or at least make the pretense thereof. Defend yourself!"

The trident stabbed out, the crowd roared sadistically, and Bill parried it and stepped away. Art jumped aside to dodge the hurled net.

"Verily, that's the stuff. We must carry this mock battle across the arena to the royal box. Take that, knave!"

The sword thrust grazed Bill's side and his jacket tore when he yiped and pulled away from the cold steel. You can bet the mob really liked that.

"Easy! You want to hurt me?"

"Verily, nay. But as is spake in rude parlance we

must make it look good. Attack! Attack!"

Steel rang against steel and the vulgar mob went wild with excitement. Howling happily when the net caught the king's leg. Howling unhappily when he escaped. Clash and clash it went until the battle was just under the royal box.

"This is . . . it!" Art panted. "There is an emergency exit from the arena just under the box. Guarded by that sentry. We escape that way—after you kill me."

Clash of steel, roar of crowd, whisper of confusion.

"If I kill you—how do we escape?"

"Pretend to kill me, addlepate! Entrap me in your net, then thrust down twixt arm and chest. As in all the bad plays."

"Gotcha. Here goes."

Fast as a striking cobra the net lashed out to entrap and engulf his opponent. Only Bill wasn't very good at net throwing and Art had to dive forward to be caught by it. Pulling up the edge so that it enwrapped him.

"Get on with it, knave!" he hissed at Bill who stood there blinking. "Fall upon me and seek the verdict of the crowd."

A little rehearsal might have helped, but with this audience who cared. Bill jumped forward and Art fell before his onslaught, his trident enmeshed, where he had enmeshed it himself, in the net. Bill seized his opponent's limp wrist and pressed it to the ground, then knelt on his chest. Feeling slightly ridiculous he raised his sword ready to strike—and turned to the crowd.

They were really buying this simpleminded act. Leaping to their feet and calling out for death, all their thumbs pointing to the ground. Bill looked on all sides and all the thumbs were down. Then looked up at Pediculus who thrust down the cruelest thumb of all.

"Finish him off," he shouted. "We've got plenty of acts to follow."

Bill plunged the sword down as he had been instructed. Art's body arched in the throes of death, then was still. The crowd went wild. Bill pulled the sword free and marched to stand before the royal box. All eyes were upon him. Which was a good thing since the king was really tangled in the net and having a hard time getting free. Bill caught this out of the corner of his eye and leapt forward brandishing his weapon, crying out. A distraction was very much in order.

"Hail, Centurion Pediculus, all hail. Hail!"

"Hail, hail, sure," Pediculus muttered looking at his program, then glancing back to Bill. "Say—how come there's no blood on your sword?"

"Because I wiped it on the corpse's clothes."

"I didn't see you wipe it," he leaned forward eyes spinning. "In fact—I don't even see the corpse!"

"This way!" Art called out, pushing aside the guard he had struck down and kicking open the door with the red EXIT sign above it.

Bill did not have to be asked twice. Art dived through it with Bill right on his heels. They ran down the long, curving tunnel, feebly lit by the sunlight that trickled down through the cracks in the bleachers above. Broken nutshells and olive pits also trickled down on them. Now there was the rumble of feet and angry cries of frustration and rage. Behind them there was a crash as the exit door was torn open and armed soldiers burst through.

"Run, varlet—run! As if the very . . . hounds of hell were upon your heels!"

"They are!" Bill gasped at the fierce howling behind them.

There was a glimmer ahead and Bill saw the light at the end of the tunnel. The wooden door there had been swung open—and an armed man barred their way!

"We are lost!" Bill wailed.

"We are saved! Yon warrior is of my band!"

"Hail, Arthur," the warrior shouted, raising his glistening sword.

"Hi, Mordred. Did you bring the horses?"

"Forsooth, verily."

"That's the good knight. Avaunt—we jaunt!"

An armed band of soldiers milled about beneath the trees. Arthur bounded athletically into the saddle of his horse while Bill was heaved into the saddle of another horse by Mordred, who leapt up behind him. They were off at full gallop over the greensward before the first of their pursuers burst out through the doorway.

But their escape had not gone unnoticed. All of the army was at their heels now, shouting and cursing. And shooting off arrows, hurling spears. But two of the men in heavy armor rode to the rear of the posse so that the arrows and swords bounced harmlessly from their metal protection. And, it must be added, from the horses as well since they wore steel haunch and hock protectors, as well as chainmail leggings and, since they were stallions, riveted steel jockstraps. Everything had been planned down to the last detail.

Along the road they galloped towards the castle —and the drawbridge was coming down! It crashed to the ground as the first horse raised its first hoof. Down the hoof came on solid wood, and down came the other hooves right behind it. A thunderous rumble rumbled as they galloped across the draw-bridge—which rose instantly when the last tail had flicked safely by. The attackers could only rage at the moat's edge while the defenders pissed themselves with laughter in the crenellations above.

The horsemen reined up in the courtyard in a clatter of hooves and a spray of horsesweat. Bill slid to the ground and Art, here known better as King Arthur, strode forward and clasped his hand with friendship.

"Welcome stranger, welcome to Avalon."

"That's all very well," Bill said. "I appreciate the favor. But what about my friends—we can't just leave them back there to die." Then he had a hideous sinking feeling.

"Or—perhaps they are dead already!"

CHAPTER 21

"ALLAY YOUR FEARS, NEW COMRADE BILL. Forsooth, knew I not that the brouhaha at the arena, and yeah verily the escape and chase, would create a great diversion? And draw off the troops. Therefore my boldest knights sallied forth through a secret tunnel known not to the enemy. From a place of hiding they did perceive events—and were to fall upon the weakened soldiery and free your friends. Avaunt! We shall ascend and determine ye outcome of events."

Arthur, who was in pretty good shape, took the tower steps two at a time with Bill right behind him. They emerged at the top to find an old geezer with a pointed hat waiting for them.

"All hail, Arthur the King. Hail, hail!" he hailed.

"And hail to you, good Merlin. What dost thou report?"

"I dost report that I have gazed at yon magic mirror and have followed ye progress of all that transpired below."

Bill examined the magic mirror and nodded approvingly. "Not a bad little reflecting telescope. Did you grind the mirror yourself?"

Merlin raised one shaggy white eyebrow, combed his fingers through his flowing beard and spoke.

"My liege, yeah verily, who is this weisen-heimer?"

"He hite Bill and is the prisoner I salved from yon arena. And what of the other captives?"

"Verily I perceived events with . . ." he glared at Bill, "my magic mirror. Your puissant knights did hurtle to the attack, did brast their spears on the oafish defenders who didst flee in panic, did thus free the prisoners."

"Bully! So come dear friends, we shall below to partake of sweetmeats and fine wines, thus we celebrate this day."

The fine wine sounded like a fine idea to Bill and he trod on Merlin's robe in his haste. The hall, when they reached it, was filled with tall blokes in metal armor, which clashed and squeaked as they stamped about bragging at the top of their lungs.

"Did thoust see my lance brast upon his pate?"

"Impaled three of the buggers at one time!"

"Not that I'm keeping score, but . . ."

"Bill!" a familiar friendly voice called out and Meta pushed her way through the troops. There were shouted complaints as she walked on someone's spurs, then knocked aside a corpulent chainmailed knight. Warm muscular arms engulfed Bill, burning sensuous lips crushed his and his blood pressure mounted to match his rising body temperature.

"What hite this fair maid?" Arthur's voice spake from a great distance and Bill surfaced to make the intros.

"Meta, Arthur. Arthur, Meta. Arthur is king around here."

"Shake, Art. I like your pad. And thanks for sending the troops to our rescue. If there is anything to do in return—just ask."

The king's eyeballs grew red with lust as he clasped her hand, shouldering Bill aside. "There be one thing," he said hoarsely.

"Arthur, you must introduce me to these delightful people." The words were commonplace, yet dark with menace. The king dropped Meta's hand as if it were a hot poker, turned and bowed.

"Guenevire, my queen, what dost thou here so distant from your privy chambers?"

"Keeping my eye on you." She kept an eye on Bill too, looking him up and down and smiling.

"I'm Bill, this is Meta," he said to the ravishing redhead.

"My pleasure, queen," Meta said insincerely. "When we get to know each other better you *must* let me know who dyes your hair..."

"Hearken to me, all ye here!" Arthur called out quickly before things got even more out of hand. "All assembled here to bid welcome to our guests, salved but recently from pagan hands. Kind guests to greet Sir Lancelot, Sir Gawain, Sir Mordred..." and a lot more like that. Not to be oneupsmanshipped, Bill introduced his lot, ranks, serial numbers and all. Plenty of handshaking went on after that and Bill was more than glad to grab the glass of wine the waiter brought to him. A number of toasts followed, and to hold the wine down they were served sweetmeats. Which turned out to be sugar-glazed sparrows. Which wouldn't have been too bad if they had taken the feathers off first. Then the knights trampled out to change armor, the ladies went off to powder their noses. The freed prisoners dropped into chairs around a large, round table that had been pushed up against the wall during the festivities. Arthur rapped on the table with the handle of his dagger.

"Ye meeting will come to order. Newfound military friends, tis not by chance we gather here today. Merlin shall spake to you of what befell, befalls and shall be befalling. Merlin."

The spattering of handclapping died away as Merlin climbed to his feet.

"Now look you," he said, a touch of the Rhondda to his words. "Good King Arthur has had it up to here, and above, with the pestilential Roman Legions. This kingdom does fine, taxes roll in, so do a few serfs' heads when the taxes are late—but that's what feudalism is all about isn't it? But I digress. Without outside interference we could grow our corn, brast a few skulls in the tourneys, the peasantry would tug their forelocks and all would be right with the world. But it is not. Every time things seem to be going right—here come the legions again. They besiege the castle, fire off their ballistae and arbolasts and generally play silly buggers until they get tired and go home. Which is fine for them. I suppose it keeps their simplistic economy turning over, bread and circuses and all that crap. But what about us? Taxes go up as we have to buy more oil for boiling. The work on the bridges and nunneries has to stop when we haul the stonemasons back here to repair the walls. And do you know how long this has been going on? Since the dawn of history, that's how long."

"And soon shall end, that I have swore."

"Right, Arthur, end, sure, where was I?" The interruption had put Merlin off his mellifluous stride. He knocked back a beaker of mead, hummed a few bars of "Men of Harlech" to clear his throat and managed to work up enthusiasm anew. His voice bellowed forth until the corbels rang.

"But no more! Arthur, the king, as you have just

heard, is fed up to here with the situation. Spies have been sent forth. The ones that weren't caught and crucified have returned. Here is what they have discovered."

The silence deepened, every eye on him now, even Arthur's; he had heard the story before but was still entranced by Merlin's magic words. Meta, nose well powdered, slipped in through the door and joined the ranks. Another sip of mead and Merlin was off and running.

"They are pagans all, but this we have always known. Divining the future in goat's guts, burning incense to Mercury and Saturn, seeking fertility with sacrifices to Minerva, paying homage to Jupiter and all the other pantheonic puke. But, boy bach, I ask you— which god is missing? I see only bafflement in your eyes denoting either bad memory or a rotten classical education. Then I will tell you. Mars is missing!"

They all clapped loudly at this, not knowing why except it seemed to be a big point to Merlin. Then they quickly knocked back some wine as he went on.

"Mars, god of war. Certainly of great importance to this warlike tribe. My spies were too chicken to penetrate deeper into the country, to follow the Centurions when they made their secret way past the mountains. But I followed them there myself, for there are no secrets that can be hidden from Merlin! Disguised as an old man with a white beard I tottered after them until I discovered it, past the furthermost hill, at the cliff's edge where the plateau ends—there I found it!"

"The best part comes next," King Arthur said, eyes glowing, fingers clutching the pommel of his sword in anticipation.

"Do you know what *it* was? I will tell you. It was the Temple of Mars! Carved into solid rock, with marble columns, figured lintel and an altar set before it upon which the sacrifices and offerings were placed. And the officers themselves carried the offerings, not a legionary in sight, which will give you some idea how secret and important all this is. When they had made the sacrifices they fell back, almost with fear—and lo! they had damned good reason!

"Night fell, although it was still day. Thunder rumbled and lightning crashed. Then a mysterious glow filled the air and it could be seen that the offerings were gone. And then, in a very impressive encore, Mars himself spoke. And that raised the hairs on the neck and emptied the bladder let me assure you. Nor was Mars content with a couple of prophecies or a weather report. That celestial sod ordered them to start the war again! That's where the trouble is coming from. Those lazy legionnaires and corpulent centurions are more than happy to sit around throwing slaves to the lions and getting smashed on cheap plonk. But, oh no, that's not good enough for Mars. Get the war moving he says, build ballistae, step up the draft, invade . . ."

Merlin was so carried away that he began to froth and vibrate. Meta sprang to his aid and, with Bill's help, settled him in his chair again and poured a beaker of mead into his mouth. Arthur nodded with grim understanding.

"There you have it within ye nutshell. We must do battle with the pagan gods if we are to free ourselves from this endless war."

"Not a bad idea," Praktis nodded. "And you have just the troops to do it. Armored cavalry, sudden attack, outflank the armies. Bam—the job is done."

"Would it were but so, puissant Admiral. But, verily, 'tis not. My strong and fearless knights quail before the gods and seek shelter beneath their beds."

Merlin had recovered and nodded his head furiously. "Superstitious saps, that's what they are. Full of noble words—Verily wouldst I lay down my life for mine liege lord! Verily my flabby buttocks! One lightning bolt from the temple and they would run a furlong. There is no help there. Craven and shivering—despite the fact that I offered them complete religious protection as well!"

Merlin seized up a leather bag and dumped its contents out onto the round table. "Look at this! Garlic by the ton. More crosses than you could find in a dozen monasteries. Crucifixes filled with holy water. Relics by the binful, saints' bones by the bagful, a piece of the True Cross, bilge pump off the Ark—everything. And what do they say when I show them this? I think I may have a previous engagement. None of them will go—not even the king."

"Verily, I would sally forth on the quest were it not that the pressing business of rule doth stay me. Heavy hangs the head that bears the crown."

"Yeah, sure," Merlin muttered, far from being conned but careful not to sink into lese majesty. "So where are we now? We have a menace to the realm, identified and located and ready to be knocked out. By one old man? You must be joking. I got powers, sure, but I need brawn and a few battle-axes behind me."

"Which is where we come in," Bill said, aware now that their rescue had not been that altruistic.

"You've been peeking at my cards. I saw you land through my telescope—magic mirror that is. You were brought in by flying dragon and, being Welsh, I greatly appreciated that. I said, King, I said, those are the toughies we need. Strangers, not afraid of the gods." He stopped and looked at them piercingly. "You are not superstitious—are you?"

"I'm a Fundamentalist Zoroastrian," Bill said humbly.

"Get on with it," Praktis snarled. "Let's hear the proposition first, then we get out of it afterwards."

"There is no more to be said. Good King Arthur freed you from the Legions. You will be armed and you will follow me to the Temple of Mars where we will buy Mars off with an offering or two."

"Sounds simple enough," Cy sneered. "But what if we don't go?"

"That's easy. You go—back to the circus. And we will donate a few hungry lions to the festivities."

"Be ye of good cheer," King Arthur advised, pulling rank. "And be ye advised that ye honours list is going in soonest. Verily a knighthood or two, maybe a garter and a CBE, lurketh in ye future."

They were less than impressed by the generosity of the offer. "We would like to talk this over among ourselves," Meta said.

"Of course. Take your time. Take a whole hour." Merlin put a sandglass on the table and turned it over. "The choice is yours. A journey to the temple—or back to the Big Top."

CHAPTER **22**

"IT'S ALWAYS BOWB-YOUR-BUDDY WEEK,"
Bill sniffed pathetically.

"It was the dog—if only I hadn't whistled to
the dog," Captain Bly whined.

"I could use some dope," Cy sussurated.

"It's harvest time back on the farm," Wurber
whimpered.

Meta curled her lip in disgust and Praktis nodded agreement. "If I were still in command I would
shake you miserable lot out of your depression
quickly enough. But, being just one of the boys now
all I can do is suggest that we stop weeping in our
beer and find a way out of this."

He looked out of the window and sought succor; but it was a straight drop to the rocks below.
Meta tried the door but Arthur had locked it behind
him when they left.

"Why don't we do just what they asked?" Bill
said brightly, then cowered beneath the barrage of
angry glares. "Listen—let me finish before you glare
me to death. I was going to say that there was no
easy way out of this castle. And even if there were
the Legion is still there to cope with. So we go along
with this screwball plan. We get weapons and all and

slip out of here—along with one ancient Welsh-man."

"I read you loud and clear," Praktis chortled. "Henceforth you will be known as First Lieutenant Bill. We get well clear of the castle and the Legions, knock the old boy on the head—then trot off armed and free and on our own!"

There was a thud as the last grain of sand dropped through the sandglass and, at the same instant, the door rattled and opened. King Arthur entered.

"What sayest thou?"

"We sayest yay," they saidest.

"If ye die it will be in the noblest of causes. Get thee hence to the armourers!"

They were fitted with armor, chainmail, helms, halberds, dirks, daggers, crossbows, swords, shields and relief tubes. "I can't move," Bill muffled inside his helmet.

"As long as your sword arm is free it matterest not," the armorer said, hammering a loose rivet into place on Praktis's helmet.

"I've gone deaf—knock that off!" the admiral howled, taking one staggering step then crashing to the floor. "I can't get up."

"Unaccustomed as thee are to armor, perhaps less might be in order." The armorer signaled his assistants. "Strip them down a bit so they can move."

After about a ton of armor had been cast aside they could walk easily—though they creaked. The old oil can put that right and they were quaffing a bit of wine for the road when Merlin, similarly armored, came in riding on a donkey.

"Do we get to ride too?" Bill asked.

"Shank's mare, boyo, good for the muscle tone. We exit through this secret tunnel that will bring us out in the hills beyond the attacking Legion."

"Sounds great," Praktis said, and they all winked wildly at each other and chuckled behind their hands when Merlin turned away. Lit torches were handed to them, a barred door swung open, and they followed Merlin down the dank, water-dripping tunnel. And it was a long tunnel. They seemed to be staggering on forever, the air growing musty and foul, their torches going out one by one. When the last torch was flickering its last Praktis called out to Merlin.

"This is a silly question, I know—but when this torch snuffs it, how do we find our way?"

"Fear not—for Merlin is a wizard. The torch dies. But I have this magic crystal ball to lighten the darkness. Abra Cadabra!"

He removed the sphere from the bag fixed before him and held it high. It glowed weakly, then brightened when he shook it. Bill looked close, then whispered to Meta.

"Some magic. He's got a crummy old fishbowl full of fireflies."

"I heard that!" Merlin shouted. "But it's more than you have, Snoopy, and it will get us out of here."

The end of the tunnel finally appeared and they emerged into a shadowed glade. Filled with King Arthur's troops.

"An honor guard," Merlin smirked. "To see that you all do the honorable thing and don't try to go AWOL before we reach the Temple of Mars."

Their response was only silence and dark looks. He cackled with senile hilarity and led the way. The reluctant volunteers followed him and the troops followed them. They marched all that day, through forest, wooded canyons, dry river bottoms, along bubbling brooks and through glacier-worn foothills. It was a long hot march and at its end they dropped gratefully into the soft grass of a meadow as the sun slipped from sight.

"I'm thirsty," Cy said.

"Water in that stream." Merlin pointed the way. "Five guards will go with you."

"When do we eat?" Bill asked.

"Now. Sergeant, pass out the hardtack."

Each piece had ABC stamped into it, standing for the Avalon Bread Company, and it must have been stamped in before they were baked. Or annealed, or petrified, or whatever. Because the tooth had not been grown in the jaw not yet born that could bite a piece from an Avalonian hardtack. It had to be pounded between two rocks, strong rocks, because weak ones broke before the hardtack did. Any pieces of hardtack that splintered off might become edible if soaked in water. They muttered and pounded and glared at Merlin who was eating cold roast swan and washing it down with malmsey.

For two days they marched in this fashion, until they entered a dark and ominous valley. A giant rift was carved in the rock as though by a giant's ax. The valley dripped with water from hidden springs, the stone walls were covered with foul lichen. "Not too far now," Merlin said cheerily. "This valley goes by the quaint local name of Descensus Avernus. Which can be translated roughly as You go in but you don't go out."

"Company—halt!" the commander of their

guards ordered. "Where doth this dank valley go, honored wizard?"

"It leadeth to the Temple of Mars."

"Verily! Then we shall remaineth here and guard your rear. Go with our blessings!"

"Thanks. I'm surprised I got you this far. Wait here then for our return. And, postus scriptus, if I don't come back with this lot, should they return alone, you can use them as targets for your bowmen."

"Verily, as you say!"

Merlin squinted up at the sky. "A couple of hours yet before it gets dark. Let's get this over with. Here."

He handed down a heavy bag that had been lashed to the back of the saddle.

"What's this?" Meta asked, hefting its weight.

"The religious safeguards that I showed you."

"Leave them with these cowardly troops," Praktis said, superiority dripping from his fingertips. "Might help their morale."

"If you say so. But first..." Merlin rooted about in the bag and dug out a cross, a six-pointed star, a crescent and a piece of garlic. "I don't hold with superstition myself but it doesn't hurt to hedge your bets. Onward."

They followed him in gloomy silence until a turn in the canyon took them out of sight of the troops.

"Let's hold it right here," Praktis said and they ground to a halt.

"I did not order a stop," Merlin said.

"But I did. If we are going all the way with you—and looking at the steepness of the rock wall I would say we had little choice—just what is your plan of action?"

"To go to the temple."

"And then?"

"Call upon Mars to appear and partake of our gifts and offerings."

"What gifts and offerings?"

"All that hardtack you've been shlepping. It's not good for anything else. Then when he takes our gifts we get him on our side. Then he can stop issuing orders for war. Simple."

"Simple minded," Bill said. "Why should Mars do that?"

"Why not? Gods are always interceding in mankind's affairs. It just depends who gets the bribe in first."

"I'm not intrigued by this lecture on comparative theology," Meta said. "The damp is getting into my chainmail and I'm going to rust solid if we don't move. All this jaw-jaw is accomplishing exactly nothing. Let us find the temple and play it by ear after that. Move."

They moved. And when they did, from the chasm ahead, they heard the beat of drums and the distant call of bugles.

"Listen!" Bill said. "What's that?"

"The Temple of Mars," Merlin intoned. "Prepare to meet thy destiny!"

They went on, slower and slower, hands on sword pommels, fingers plucking nervously at daggers and morning-stars. But what good would physical weapons be against the power of the gods?

The martial music sounded louder—and there it was! One last turn of the valley revealed the white marble of the temple. The altar for the offerings stood before it, and behind the altar steps led up to the dark opening of the sanctum sanctorum. They walked in silence, on tiptoe, as though afraid of disturbing the god within the temple, slowly approaching the mable altar. Which was empty of anything other than the splatters of bird droppings and an old apple core.

"The offerings," Merlin whispered as he climbed creaking from the saddle. "On the altar."

When the hardtack dropped onto the stained marble the music instantly stopped. They did too, frozen in apprehension as the darkness in the temple entrance changed, writhed with motion—and a great black cloud boiled forth. There was a clatter of hooves as the donkey galloped away. Then the voice! It didn't speak but thundered like a breaking storm, rolling out of the temple.

"Who goes there? What mortals are these who face the wrath of mighty Mars?"

"Merlin, world-famous wizard of Avalon."

"I know you, Merlin. You dabble in the arcane arts and think to control the powers of darkness."

"My hobby, great Mars. I also go to church every Sunday. Now I, and my comrades, have come to do you homage and bring you great gifts and beseech your godly aid in our endeavors..."

"Great gifts!" the mighty voice bellowed. **"These inedible wafers you dare put before Mars!"** A great gust of wind burst from the temple, blowing the hardtack away and knocking them all to the ground.

And this wasn't all! The clouds and darkness billowed and thundered, redshot now with the fires of hell, and within their murky midst a face took shape. Ugly and scowling, wearing a helmet with a spike on the top and skulls all about. When Mars opened his mouth to bellow at them they could see that all of his teeth were the size, and shape, of tombstones.

"I reject your puny and inedible gifts. You risk death for your temerity—"

"How about this then?"

Merlin held up a gold bar he had taken from his wallet and it gleamed in the bursts of lightning.

"That's a bit more like it!" Mars boomed. **"On the altar with it. Any more where that came from?"**

"Verily. Here is a pearl and silver pin for a gent's cloak, a diamond garter for the woman who has everything, a smart tie pin set with rubies and moonstones."

"Moonstones, good. Diana will like them."

"I am glad that mighty Mars is glad. Therefore I request a boon."

"Speak. What is it that you wish."

" 'Tis simple, a small thing. Stop the war. Order the Legion back to their barracks."

"What is this, mortal? Ask Mars, God of War, to stop the war? Never!"

A thunderbolt shot out of the mouth of Mars and blasted the ground at their feet, blowing a smoking hole in the ground. They dived aside as Mars boomed his wrath above them.

"I should destroy you as well with my heavenly thunderbolts. The war goes on. Leave —or you die. In return for your offerings I give you your lives. No more. Begone!"

When the lightning hit Bill had dived for cover and plastered himself against the wall of the temple.

The entrance was close by and the roiling fog not as thick here. He crept forward and poked his head around the marble column. And looked. Then looked a lot more. Only when he felt himself looked out did he creep back and join the others.

"Great Mars," Merlin implored. "If not an end to the war—how about a cease-fire for a few months until the crops are in?"

"Never!" Lightning flared and exploded around him. "Begone now or you die! The count-down to destruction is resumed. Nine . . . eight . . . seven . . ."

"We hear you, Mars, no problem!" Bill shouted. "Going back down the valley now. Been nice to meet you. Bye-bye."

Merlin hesitated but the rest were happy to leave. Until Bill waved them down, put finger to lips for silence, and crept back along the temple walls.

"He's cracked up," Praktis said.

"Shut up and look!" Meta punctuated her words with a sharp elbow in his ribs. Bill was at the entrance to the temple now—standing and stepping through it! He waved them after him. In silent wriggle they wriggled his way. While Mars boomed and bellowed.

"Four . . . three . . . And you are gone! And don't come back, miserable Merlin—nor any of your henchmen. Only death at the hands of mighty Mars awaits you here!"

Bill walked into the temple and the others followed him.

"Look," he said. "Won't you just look at that!"

CHAPTER 23

THE INTERIOR OF THE TEMPLE HAD BEEN carved roughly from the rock, with the marks of the drills and chisels still visible. Spiderwebs filled the corners and dry leaves littered the floor. Elegant it was not. Right beside the entrance a smoke generator was pumping out smoke. This rose into the air in a dense cloud. The image of Mars's face was being projected onto the cloud by a movie projector to the rear. His voice echoed and laughed from matched Wharfdale speakers, complete with woofers and tweeters.

"**Ho-ho-ho!**" the loudspeakers thundered.

"Just what the bowb is going on here?" Praktis asked, staring in amazement at the display.

"A fake is going on here," Cy said. "The Great God Mars is just a bag of electronic tricks. But who is pressing the buttons?"

Bill pointed to a curtained alcove to the rear of the temple and they all smiled wickedly, drew their swords, and tiptoed over to it.

"Ready?" Bill whispered and they nodded viciously. "Then—here goes!"

The dark curtain was on tracks just like a shower curtain. In fact it was a shower curtain Bill realized as he whisked it aside. They stared—and their swords slowly dropped to their sides.

Because inside the curtain was an instrument console with dials, a TV screen, and projecting brass levers. "Ho-ho-ho!" the little bald-headed man said into the microphone and behind them **"Ho-ho-ho!"** boomed the amplified voice of Mars.

"We have a little of the old Ho-ho-ho for you as well," Bill said.

"Be with you in a moment," the man muttered, feverishly working the levers. "Damned smoke generator won't extinguish . . . Arrrrgh!"

He *arrrrghed!* in shocked horror as he suddenly realized he was no longer alone. He spun about, fell back against the console, bulged his eyes, gasped with shock and clutched his chest.

"Who . . ." he gurgled, "are you?"

"That's funny, Pops," Praktis said. "We were just going to ask you the same question."

"You brutes," Meta said, brushing past them and taking the old man by the arm. "Can't you see how awful he looks? Do you want to give him a heart attack? There, there, take it easy." She pulled over the wooden chair that stood beside the console and eased him into it. "Sit down. No one's going to hurt you."

"That's arguable," Merlin said, striding forward, sword raised. "If he's the voice of Mars he's the sod who has been causing all the trouble for Avalon!"

Bill reached out and pinched Merlin's funny-bone. He squawked loudly and the sword dropped from his numbed fingers. "Let's get some answers to some questions first, before the swords start swishing," he said, then turned to the man in the chair.

"Explain. Who are you—and what are you doing here?"

"It had to come some day, that was certain," the man muttered. "In a way—I'm glad it's over with at last. Climbing those steps was killing me." He raised moist eyes to Meta. "On top of the console, my dear, if you don't mind. Brandy. Just a bit in the glass."

As he sipped the color returned to his face. Then he had a moment's reprieve before he faced his captors again because the captors were passing the bottle from hand to hand and gurgling it down. By the time it got to Merlin there was about a single shot left; he scowled and drained it, hurled the bottle aside.

"Explain, varlet!"

"The name is not Varlet. I am the wizard of Zog."

"Aye, bach, and I'm the wizard of Avalon. Get on with it."

"It's a long, long story."

"We've got all the time in the world. Speak!"

He spoke:

THE WIZARD OF ZOG'S TALE

It all goes back a long, long time. Centuries at least. I found the log book, but the entries were all very old. And what with no calendar here, no change of seasons worth mentioning, it's hard to keep track of time. But I managed to piece the story together, from what my father told me and what I read in the log book of the spaceship. An immigrant ship I gather, the SS Zog, carrying settlers to a distant world. There was trouble aboard, the details are not clear, some tragedy. Perhaps there was a mutiny, or the beer ran out, or the toilets exploded, perhaps all of them. There are dark hints of strange events. In any case, the Zog was diverted and landed on this planet. Was destined never to leave. And, as you see, the settlers remain here to this day.

There was trouble from the very first. The ship's captain was named Gibbons and I am descended from him for I am named Gibbons as well. The captain wanted to organize the settlers in his own way, but the first mate, an evil chap named Mallory, wouldn't go along with it. He had his own ideas how a civilized society should be organized. He took his followers and left, marched to the far side of the plateau and founded Avalon.

My grandfather was glad to see them go, for that is written in the log. Medieval rubbish he called their culture, very inferior to the Glories that were Rome. His followers settled on this end of the plateau and thrived in the salubrious climate. There is also something written in the log, scarcely legible now, about a third group that were traveling steerage. They would have nothing to do with either group and marched off to the Barthroomian plateau and have not been heard of since.

And that's the way it has been down through the centuries. Captain Gibbons knew that the trappings of science and technology were not needed for a simple agrarian society so he withdrew here to oversee his charges. The Temple of Mars was built, all of the equipment secretly installed, and so has it been down through the ages. The Roman Legions do their thing, Arthur and his Avalonians do theirs —and a watchful Mars watches and keeps order.

* * *

There was silence after Zog Gibbons had finished speaking, as they digested his words—and the brandy. It was Merlin who spoke first.

"I appreciate the history lesson. But don't appreciate in the slightest your keeping the war going. Why?"

"Why? You have to ask why?"

"Yes," they all chorused. Zog started to rise from the chair but was pressed back. There was no escape. He sighed heavily, and spoke.

"Survival I suppose, and the easy life. And playing god. It is heady stuff to throw thunderbolts and order everyone around. It beats working for a living. The sacrifices include the best wine, roast rack of lamb, honey-dipped mice, everything. I like that. I also like keeping the war going. If I didn't someone would catch wise as to what was happening. There would be peace and prosperity for all. And progress. Oh how I hate that word! Progress was what caused all of mankind's problems. My ancestor, Captain Gibbons was firm on that. I have read his writings and agree with every word. With progress comes politicians, graduated income tax, advertising agencies, fem lib, pollution, all the things that make modern life so hideous. Better the Golden Age of Rome. No decline and fall here!"

"I'm beginning to think that this guy is crackers," Praktis said.

"Don't knock it—it's a good scam," Cy said, then pointed to a thick cable that ran along the wall. "This your electricity supply?"

Zog nodded. "And mighty precious it is too, although the voltage drops slowly all of the time. It will take me a month to recharge the batteries after shooting off those two thunderbolts. All your fault, meddling in other peoples' affairs."

"Before we get too maudlin," Merlin growled, "let us kindly remember who is the master meddler in other peoples' affairs around here."

"What interests me more than other peoples' affairs," Bill said, "are electrical affairs. Where does the electricity come from—and where does that power cable go?"

"You took the words right out of my mouth," Cy said. Zog struggled to his feet.

"Follow me," he said, "and all will be revealed."

He shuffled from the temple and Praktis shuffled right along behind him, with a firm grip on his collar, just to make sure he didn't shuffle off to Buffalo or some such. The cable ran up the wall to thick insulators set in the solid stone. Then it looped out of the temple and up the valley. They followed it until the valley ended abruptly in a cliff. The cable went over the edge and vanished from sight. They all walked forward carefully and peered over. They were at the very edge of the plateau. The stony walls fell away to the desert below, the trackless wastes of sand. But there were tracks now. Just beside them stairs had been carved in the stone and led down to the desert. From the bottom of the stairs a path made a track across the trackless wastes. It lead directly to the open airlock of the spaceship.

"The SS Zog—it's still here!" Bill gasped.

"Of course it's still here," Praktis growled. "Where else would you expect it to be . . ."

"Whoever moves gets it between the eyes," the voice behind them ordered. "Drop the swords and turn about, real slow."

CHAPTER 24

THEY PUT THEIR SWORDS DOWN AND turned slowly to see the young man standing in the rocks above them. With a sneer on his lips and a gun in his hand.

"This is an ion pistol," he said, "that shoots out a deadly beam of ions. And until you have been ionized you don't know what real pain is, screaming and writhing and wishing that you were dead." He grinned in sadistic anticipation and licked his lips.

"Who the hell are you," Praktis said.

"I'm the guy with the ion pistol!" he laughed crudely.

"This is my son, Young Zog," Old Zog said. "The heir to the temple, Mars in the making." He didn't sound too enthusiastic about it either.

"Heir my arse!" Young Zog shouted. "I'll be dead of waiting by the time you retire. And PS, Daddy-o, you will notice that the pistol is pointed at you as well. Getting yourself captured—you are no longer fit to be Mars! The old Mars is dead—long live the new Mars!" The spittle really flew at this one and Old Zog shook his lowered head.

"You aren't fit for the job, my boy. I can admit it now. That's why I stayed on long past my retirement age. You are too headstrong, reckless..."

"You betcha!" Young Zog cried out and pulled the trigger and ionized a chunk of rock out of the cliff's edge. "This is it, folks! Those of you who are religious can utter a quick prayer to the god or gods of your choice. Then let the ionizing begin!"

"Oh, I feel I shall faint with horror!" Meta said, closing her eyes and fainting with horror, making a loud crash as she hit the ground.

"My boy, don't say things like that! You would not kill these innocent people."

"Just like that, Pops! And you too as well. So say bye-bye and prepare to meet your ancestors!"

He stepped forward, raised and aimed the gun. But before he could pull the trigger Meta, judo champ three years running of the LAGTAA, showed her judo stuff by latching onto his ankle as he passed. He yiked once as his legs were pulled out from under him, the gun dropped as he was chopped on the arm, he dropped as he was chopped in the jaw.

"Thanks, Meta," Bill said with great sincerity.

"Someone had to do something—you jokers were just standing there while this maniac got on with his ionizing."

"He is a poor, misunderstood boy," Zog said, staggering over and kneeling at his son's side.

"The kid's a loony," Praktis declared. "Tie him up before he comes to and tries to take over again. I'll hold this." He scooped up the ion pistol. "Are there any more screwballs loose around here, Zog? The truth now."

"My only son, my only child, the apple of my eye," Zog wept as he folded up his cloak and tucked it under Young Zog's head as a pillow. "My own fault, spoiled him rotten. It went to his head, all the power that would be his. That is not to be, not to be . . ."

"Oh yes it is," the voice said. "All of you, get back from him. Up against the rock wall."

The gray-haired woman had climbed the stone steps behind them, when they weren't looking, and now pointed a nasty looking rifle at them.

"Is that an ion rifle, Ma'am?" Bill asked politely.

"You bet your sweet kazoo, sonny. One touch of the trigger and a ravening stream of ions blasts forth destroying all before it."

"That's nice," Bill said, closing the faceplate on his helmet and stepping forward. "Would you mind handing it to me before someone gets hurt?"

"That's going to be you, kiddo, if you take another step!"

Bill took the other step and the ravening ions ravened forth. Meta screamed as his body was outlined with fire as the ions really ravened.

He took another step, clutched the ion rifle, tore it from the woman's grip and threw it over the cliff.

"You're alive!" Meta gasped.

"He should be," Cy said, "because he knows his physics better than you do. Ions are electrically charged particles. Which hit his metal armor and were grounded. Simple."

"So simple I didn't see you stepping forward."

"So I'm chicken," he shrugged. "Cluck."

"My wife, Electra," Zog said.

"Any more?" Praktis asked, peering about on all sides, pistol ready.

"No more," Zog sobbed. "We had hoped for a larger family, the pitter-patter of little feet around the spaceship. But it was not to be. If the family had been larger this would never have happened. The apple of her eye, her only child, I can see it now, spoiled rotten by his mother..."

"Blame me, you impotent old bastard!" Electra screeched. "Oh how I regret the day I was sacrificed to Mars. If I had tried out for the vestal virgins I know I would have made it. But, no, my mother said. A better fate waits you, for you are of noble birth..."

"Knock it off," Praktis suggested. "Carry on the family feud when I'm not around. Let us get down to the spaceship because I am hungry and thirsty and tired of all this nonsense. It has been one long day."

"Made even more tiring by this armor," Meta said, stripping hers off and throwing it over the cliff.

They all agreed instantly and a great clanging and banging followed. Then, with Zog leading the way, they left Young Zog to the tender mercies of his mother and descended to the desert.

"I regret to say that the only thing I have to drink at the moment," Zog apologized, "is chilled sacrificial wine. I get a lot."

"I'll make the sacrifice," Bill said and smacked his lips with anticipation.

The galley of the spacer was neatly fitted out with curtains on the bulkhead, rocking chairs, fresh metal flowers and plenty of glasses. Cy drained his glass three times and belched happily as he pointed to the heavy cable that had come down the rock face and across the sand, in through the open spacelock and now vanished into the nether regions of the ship.

"Where does that go?" he asked.

"Into the nether regions of the ship," Zog said. "I know not where or why, or even how it functions. All the equipment was installed by my ancestors. I just run it. There are alarms in the valley to let me know when someone is coming. I climb the stairs, work the levers and switches and bring back the sacrifices. Speaking of that—more wine anyone?"

They all did him a favor and let him stand another round. Except for Cy who was very curious about the cable. While they got boozed he traced it across the room and into the corridor beyond. He was gone for some time, but was not missed as the sacrificial wine flowed. When he returned he gave a quick sneer at his sodden shipmates.

"Really great. First chance you have you get blasted out of your teeny-tinys."

"Sho what?" Shomeone shaid. "Why not. We've had a tough time on this planet and a little relaxation is very much in order."

"Tell me about it! No don't!" he shouted as they all started bitching at once. "That was a metaphorical statement to denote strong agreement. Can any of you lushes hear me? And understand what I am saying? Nod your heads, good, good. I wanted to tell you that I tracked the cable to the ships' atomic pile. It is still functioning after, lo, these many centuries. But it is half way to its half life, I think. A real antique. Hand operated fuel rods, crank them in and out with a wheel. And the carbon block moderators also have to be shoveled in by hand. I shoveled and cranked a bit and got the electricity flowing real nice."

"You are a technical geniushh," Praktis said thickly and they all nodded thick agreement, all except Zog that is who, because of his age and his sorrows, had drunk himself unconscious and now lay on the floor.

"Yes, thank you, I thought you would approve. Now wait for it, more to come. I found the control room for this antique, it even has a steering wheel and oil lamps, and I switched on the power there. The bulbs lit up and it all looked very nice. The radio room had the door welded shut but I broke it down. There is a FTL transmitter in there in perfect working condition."

He waited patiently as the sound waves of his voice impacted their sluggish ear drums, which then kicked the bones of the hammer, anvil and stirrup of the inner ear to life, sent neural messages slowly across alcohol laden synapses, plowed down through their ossified tissues and finally sunk home in what tiny bit of intelligence still remained in their brains...

"You **what?**" they shouted in unison, surging to their feet, glasses shattering around them, sober in a microsecond.

"Boy, if I could bottle that I would have an instant soberer-upper. And yes, you heard me right. There is an FTL signaler and it does work."

"It makes sense," Praktis said, dropping back into his rocker, red-eyed and vibrating. "The nutcase captain who started all this Roman nonsense must have sealed it up so none of his societal victims could radio for aid. But he didn't put it out of commission just in case he personally needed some help. And it had been there ever since."

"Shall we make a call?" Bill suggested and they all nodded their heads like fools and rushed out of the room on Cy's heels.

Electra Zog, leading her errant son by the ear, came in and sniffed loudly.

"Just what I should have expected. Turn my back for a second and he gets drunk on the sacrificial wine. And look at the mess!"

CHAPTER 25

ONCE THE FTL MESSAGE HAD BEEN SENT THEY hurried back to the sacrificial wine to celebrate. But even as the first glasses were being lifted in a toast to success they heard the sound.

"A spacer!" Wurber gasped.

"They are here!"

Glasses crashed to the deck as they dashed from the cabin. There was the rumble of a mighty spaceship passing overhead and they all ran to the airlock and poured out onto the desert sand. The spaceship came down low over them and Meta shouted.

"A Chinger ship! They are going to bomb us!"

They all tried to pour back into the ship as the bomb bay opened in the ship above and something dropped free.

"Too late," Meta sighed, pushing her way out of the scrum. "You don't run from an atom bomb. It has been nice knowing you, Bill, though I can't say the same for some of your friends."

"Likewise, Meta, but all is not over yet. If I am not mistaken that is not a bomb but is a message tube hanging from a tiny parachute."

He ran and reached the chute just as it hit the ground. The lid popped off and the sheet of paper dropped out into his hand.

"It's a letter," he said. "From my old friend Eager Beager who turned out to be a Chinger spy named Bgr."

"I have made his acquaintance," Meta said. "What's the spy got to say that we don't want to hear?"

"It's very interesting. Listen. Dear Bill, and companions. We are splitting this planet and it is all yours. We caught your FTL transmission asking for help and giving the planetary coordinates. So he who fights and runs away, etc. Our scouts report that a sizable fleet is already on the way, so you will be rescued soon. Signed, yours truly, Bgr. And there's a PS. He goes on—Bill, don't you and your mates forget what I said about peace. We are out for eternal peace and you should be too. End this eternal war, go for peace and prosperity. You can do it! Help us, we beg. Peace, prosperity and freedom for all!"

"Pacifist crap," Praktis said, pulling the letter from Bill's hand and tearing it into lots of little pieces. "So you have been talking sedition with the enemy, have you?"

"We were captured by them! There was no escape, until we escaped, but before that we had to listen."

"Oh, no you didn't! You could have put your hands over your ears. There have been a lot of battlefield commissions in the history of warfare, First Lieutenant. Be pleased by the fact that you are the first ever to get a battlefield decommission. Trooper. Back to the ranks. No more decent chow, officer's clubs or licensed knocking-shops for you!"

"I never had a chance to enjoy that sort of thing anyway!"

"Then you won't miss them," Praktis cackled

evilly. "War is hell, don't ever forget that."

"For the enlisted troops it is," Meta said, turning and going back into the *SS Zog* where she took another bottle of sacrificial wine from the refrigerator. "I have got to think of a way of getting a commission."

Cy and Praktis, followed by a stumbling Wurber, came in to join her and she poured them each a glassful. Captain Bly did not have to join them since he had never left. As soon as the FTL message had been sent he had dived back into the bottle and had not been out of it since. They rested their feet on his recumbent body and listened to the sounds of domestic quarrel echoing from the bowels of the ship.

"Here's to peace," Meta said and raised her glass.

"No way!" Praktis disagreed. "To war, endless war."

"You sound a bit like that fake Mars, God of War."

"Don't kid yourself—he talked a lot of sense. I would really like to fire up the old god myself, it makes a nice racket. I would do it too if Merlin hadn't slipped away when we were drunk. He'll blow the whistle and I suppose peace will descend on this happy land." He frowned and twisted his face as though he had a bad taste in his mouth.

"But just here on this plateau," Meta reminded him. "Not too far away the Barthroomians are locked in endless war. Just like us."

"You're right! I forgot—nice of you to remind me. See, good things do happen."

She drained her glass and did not bother to answer.

Outside, staring out at the trackless sand, scratching idly with his claws, Bill faced the future back in the ranks. Easy come, easy go, it had been too good to last. Anyway, at heart, he would always be an enlisted man. At heart, deeper down, he wanted really to be a civilian but that was pushing things. But all this thought was pretty heavy, not to mention depressing. What he should do was seek the traditional troopers' solution and go back into the ship and get smashed out of his teeny-tiny with all of the others. Get smashed, sing dirty songs, fall down drunk, throw up. Sounded like real fun! He turned to go when he heard the distant rumble of a spaceship. Was help on the way already? He had better get cracking on the booze before he was forcefully returned to sober military life. But the spacer arrived at supersonic speed, the boom of sound cracking across his head as it shot by close overhead and vanished. He looked up, blinking, to see the Chinger ship vanishing for a second time. But on this pass, instead of a parachute, a tiny spaceship had been dropped from its bomb bay. It zoomed about in small circle and landed almost at his feet. Then the top cracked open and a chinger poked his head out.

"Hi, Bill. I saw you were alone and I thought I would have one last word with you. Besides that, I got a present for you. We captured one of your supply ships and it was filled with spare parts for the medics. It had some nice frozen feet and I picked you out the best one. It is here, inside this automated miniaturized field hospital."

"For me, Beager! How decent of you!" Bill slobbered, stumbling forward arms extended, a tear of gratitude in his eye. Which turned to a tear of pain when Beager jumped up and punched him in the nose and knocked him backward into the sand.

"Not so fast, trooper. You want the foot you work for it. The days of the free lunch are long gone. Gee, we are learning a lot from you bowby humans."

"Work? Do what?"

"Sow dissension, pacifist propaganda, spy for us. Work hard to end the war."

"I couldn't do that—it's immoral . . ." Beager made a loud raspberry sound of contempt. Bill had the courtesy to blush. "But not quite as immoral as war itself. But, really, I couldn't be a traitor. What does the job pay?"

"A new foot."

"That's great for starters. But what about later, I mean?"

"For a loyal trooped you drive a hard, not to say, traitorous bargain. Then you are on the payroll. A thousand bucks a month and a case of booze. Is it a deal?"

"It's a . . ."

His words were drowned out by the roar of an ionizer. The ions sizzled into the sand where Beager had been standing. But you got to move fast on a 10G world. He was back in the spaceship and the lid was closed before the second shot ravened forth. It wrapped the little ship in corruscating flame, but the ship must have been coated with impervium or some such mystery of alien science so harmed it not. Rockets blasted and the spaceship soared up into the sky and vanished in the distance.

"What were you saying, Bill?" Meta asked, her voice rich with dark menace. The ion pistol pointed at him now. "I didn't catch the end of the sentence."

"It's an insult! That's what I said. An insult to

think that a loyal trooper would betray his sadistic superiors."

"That's what I thought you were going to say." She smiled warmly and slipped the weapon into her holster. "So now, while the others are getting sozzled, and before the fleet arrives, we have a good chance to strip off our clothes and make out right here on the nice warm sand."

"That's for me!" he cried with great enthusiasm, then tore great tracks in the sand with his chicken foot. He looked at it and frowned. "Is it OK with you if I change feet first? I wouldn't want to scratch you or anything."

"Well, I've waited this long," she sighed. "A little more time won't make that much difference. But get on with it, will you!"

"You betcha!" He turned the box over and found printed instructions on the other side.

Dear Bill. Press the red button to start warming it up. When the green light comes on stick your avian foot in the hole on top. Best wishes, your Chinger friend.

"That was real nice of him," Bill said, pressing the button. "For an enemy Chinger he's not a bad little guy. A lot better than some officers I know. A lot better than *all* the officers I know." The light came on and he scratched one last scratch with his claws and shoved his foot in.

He gave the yellow foot a decent burial in the desert, then wriggled and admired his new pink toes. All seven of them, but he wasn't asking any questions; never look a gift foot in the toe. He looked up at the sky where the Chinger ship had vanished.

"I really would like to help you with the peace thing, little green feller. But it's not easy. Anyway, right now I got to find a shoe. I'll think about peace some other time."

"Is that peace or a piece you are thinking about? And you can worry about the shoe later. Come here." Meta murmured the words in a highly osculatory fashion, while spinning him about and kissing him so passionately that his sperm count jumped one hundred percent.

In the name of decency—and the urgent desire to get a PG rating—we must reluctantly draw the curtain on this delicate scene of heterosexual intimacy. Let us simply observe that the sun which, as it was wont to do, sank slowly in the east and darkness descended across the trackless sand of the trackless desert and this world, for the moment at least, and only at this spot, was very positively at peace.